Archer o Heathland

———❧———

Book Four

———❧———

Chronicles

J.W. Elliot

Bent Bow
Publishing, LLC

Bent Bow Publishing
P.O. Box 1426
Middleboro, MA 02346

ISBN-13: 978-1-7336757-5-8

Cover Design by Brandi Doane McCann

If you enjoy this book, please consider leaving an honest review on Amazon and sharing on your social media sites.

Please sign up for my newsletter where you can get a free short story and more free content at: **www.jwelliot.com**

To my siblings

Book Four

Chronicles

NOTE TO THE READER

What you hold in your hands is a collection of short stories I wrote while drafting the first four full-length novels in the *Archer of the Heathland* series. My goal for the series was to craft stories that allowed bows and arrows to be used in historically accurate ways that were true to the limits and capabilities of bow and arrow technology. I also wanted to explore that world from the perspective of normal folks caught up in the rush of events they couldn't control. The stories published here helped me work out important aspects of plot and character for the series.

Each story introduces characters, conflicts, and context that appear in the novels. In part, this was an exercise to help me get to know the characters and to explore their personalities and the challenges that shaped them. These stories reveal something critical about the character's world view and where it came from as well as vital back story for each of the volumes in the series.

Blood on the Reeds introduces Owen, who appears in Book II *Betrayal* as one of the conspirators working to restore the Hassani line to the throne. It explains his motivation and sets the context for his actions in *Betrayal* and for what he will do in the last volume of the series.

The Hidden Archer reveals how and why Redmond's thinking about warfare and about Neahl's obsession to kill Salassani began to change. It also shows that, despite his being a younger brother, Redmond was as cunning and skillful as Neahl when his life was on the line. The story also introduces Mortegai, who raised Emyr and trained him to be a warrior, while also explaining why Redmond reacted the way he did to the possibility that his son might be king in Book II *Betrayal*.

War of the One-Eyed Woman provides critical background for understanding the events and context of Book III *Vengeance*. It introduces how Gwyneth became an outcast among her own people and how the downfall of the Carpentini commenced.

The Deadly Jest introduces Mara and how she became a spy and an assassin for the Order of the Rook at such a young age. In doing so, it provides our first view of the Order from the inside and reveals the competing factions that could eventually tear the Order apart. Mara will also appear in Book V *Windemere* and in two other books in the series.

The prequel to the series, *Intrigue,* is available on Amazon and cannot be included in this volume because of exclusivity agreements with Kindle Select.

This book will be followed by Book V *Windemere*, which takes a step back to look at Redmond's activities in the southland and the decisions and conflicts that drew him back to Frei-Ock Mor and the Kingdom of Coll. It sets up the conflicts that will reappear in Book VI *Renegade* in which Brion, Finola, York, and Gwyneth travel to the Kingdom of Morcia to rescue Redmond from prison.

I hope you enjoy this collection of stories that will deepen your knowledge of the heathland and the characters and conflicts that have shaped its history.

Cheers,

J. W. Elliot

TABLE OF CONTENTS

Blood on the Reeds   1

His king is dead, and Thane is on the run.

When Thane discovers that his king has been murdered in a coup and his loved ones are the next targets, he abandons his post and races to save them. He finds their manor in ruins and determines to sell his life as dearly as he can—until he discovers a frightened boy. Now he has to use all of his skill to rescue the only survivor of the massacre.

The Hidden Archer   26

In a duel to the death, only one archer can win.

Redmond stumbles upon the aftermath of an ambush while trying to warn his brother of an encircling Salassani army. When he and his companion attempt to assist the injured, they get pinned down by an archer hidden in a copse of trees. Their injured friends lay dying only a few yards away. Now Redmond has to employ all of his cunning to survive the silent menace of the hidden archer.

War of the One-Eyed Woman   45

A blinded woman, her helpless baby, and a man who wants them both dead.

Edrick's sister has been returned maimed and shamed by a neighboring Bracari chieftain with a newborn baby in her arms. When Edrick's father declares war to avenge the insult and orders Edrick to take his mother, his sister, and her baby to safety in the city of Aveen, Edrick disobeys. Now Edrick has to rush to save them from his miscalculation before the Bracari capture or kill them all.

The Deadly Jest   65

Rumors can bring spies out of the shadows.

An assassin, who doesn't like to kill, is sent on a mission by the Order of the Rook to recover a secret letter of agreement between the enemies of Coll. When she finds herself entangled in a plot to destabilize the southland, Mara has to choose to abandon the mission and save her own life or go to the aid of the innocent and complete her mission.

MAP OF
FREI-OCK ISLES

PERTH

Parsini

Perthshire Findor

NAIRN

(The Black Isle)

Navantae

LISMOR

Lismori

Arboth

Laidon
Moor

Creft

Ardell

Taurini

Bracari

Aldina Mtns.
Aldina

Keldi

Kemp
Moor

Dalm Heath

Salassani

Durk
Fife   Ballach
Fens

Aveen
Moor

Bracken
Moor

Daven
Fens

Kingdom
of the
Dunkeldi

Dale

Ghille
Heath

Dunraven

**FREI-OCK
MOR**

Heron
Moor

Aveen
Mtns.

Hackel Heath

Comrie

Skye River

**FAIR
ISLE**

Carpentini

Dunfermine

Leetwater

Mailag

Faro Forest

Bowman River

Wexford

Brechin

Duchy of Saylen

Castle
Bay

Dullwater

Alamani

Chullish

River Tilt

Spey River

Oban
Plain

Kingdom
of
Coll

Taber
Wood

Barony
of
Whit-horn

ROSYTHIA

Rosyth

Aldros

Cliffs of Prestwick

BLOOD ON THE REEDS

The rider sagged over the horse's neck as it plodded up the road toward the castle gates. The slanting light of the midsummer sun glinted off a helm that hung from the saddle horn and bounced against the horse's lathered withers. The torn shreds of the rider's purple tunic fluttered in the evening breeze.

Thane watched from the battlements for a moment as the horse seemed to slow at the sight of the castle. Then he whirled, barked a few orders, and swept down the stone stairs. The black cloak that identified him as the captain of the guard flew out behind him.

He knew he should send a messenger to the commander of the city's garrison, but some deep suspicion restrained him. A lone rider, clearly in distress wearing the King's colors here at Castle Bay, the southwesternmost city of the kingdom, was more than an oddity. It could only portend some bad fortune, and Thane would rather be prepared with more information before he called the commander.

Thane hadn't forgotten the whispered rumors the year before about the men who had attempted to kidnap Princess Eryann, nor the news of her early death—supposedly from disease. He swept under the teeth of the raised portcullis to stand beside the guards who also watched the rider approach.

"Summon a stretcher," Thane ordered. "And call the physician."

Then he strode forward to meet the rider. Thane's boots thudded hollowly on the stout boards of the drawbridge as he crossed the moat. The stench of the black water beneath lifted on the breeze. Thane grimaced and wrinkled his nose. Not for the first time, he

1

missed the fresh smell of earth and clean water he had enjoyed as a boy living on the banks of the Spey River deep in Taber Wood. He had tried to learn to enjoy city life, but he had never managed it.

The horse stopped at the edge of the drawbridge as if by command—its head bent low, almost to the ground. The rider raised his head. A shock of recognition raced through Thane.

"Rhys?" he said as he rushed to the rider's side and helped him slip from the saddle. The odor of horse sweat mingled with the coppery scent of blood.

"I found you," Rhys said. His light brown hair lay matted against his brow. His cheeks burned with a fever, and his dark eyes were wide and frightened.

Thane pulled a hand away from Rhys's back to find it covered in blood. He helped Rhys lie on the ground.

"What has happened?" Thane demanded.

He spoke more harshly than he intended. He had become too accustomed to command in the last few years.

"The King is slain," Rhys said.

A lump rose in Thane's throat. His chest grew tight. He glanced quickly to see if the guards were coming.

"How?" he choked.

"Betrayed," Rhys said. "Geric and the Duke of Saylen."

"No," Thane said. "The Duke would never betray his own family."

"He has," Rhys said. "I was the only one loyal to the King that escaped the Duke's keep."

"When?"

"Two days ago."

"The Queen?"

"Dead," Rhys said. "And the new Prince Rhodri was found strangled in her arms."

Thane sat back on his haunches and passed a hand over his head, trying to get his bearings. King Edward was dead. The King who had spared his mother from the lash and sent Thane to train with the Duke's guard. The King who had appointed Thane captain of the guard in Castle Bay where he could be closer to his aging mother and the woman he loved. The King who had stood beside Thane in battle. The King who had almost been a friend.

"They're going to Rothe Manor," Rhys said. "They're destroying the entire Hassani line."

"Esther?" Thane whispered.

Rhys nodded and swallowed. "They'll come for you, too."

"Why?"

"They fear you," Rhys said. "And your loyalty to the King and his family." He swallowed. "If you renounce the King, they may let you live."

The sound of booted feet running across the bridge echoed in the gathering darkness. Rhys grabbed Thane's hand and squeezed it with all the strength he had left.

He was weak. He had lost too much blood.

"Don't trust Commander Cyrill," Rhys said. "He's one of them. As soon as he receives word that—"

The soldiers arrived, and Thane bent low to Rhys's ear and whispered, "You were attacked by brigands on the highway." He held Rhys's gaze until he was sure the injured man understood, then rose to his feet and wiped Rhys's blood on his cloak.

"He's wounded," he said. "Take him to the hospital."

Rhys's gaze never left Thane's face as the guards lifted him onto the stretcher. Thane waited, tight-lipped, with his hand on the pommel of his sword until the guards were trooping across the bridge, one of them leading Rhys's horse. Thane turned to gaze up the road to where it disappeared into the black line of trees.

His King was dead. His commander was a traitor. And the woman he loved was in danger. Could he renounce the King? Could he betray everything he had stood for? Could he abandon the ones he loved? Thane made his decision.

He strode back across the drawbridge, edging aside the country-folk who were making their way out of the city before the gates closed. He heard the curious whisperings about the man on the stretcher, but he ignored them.

The city was settling down to another quiet evening as Thane passed through the gates and into the main street. The tradesmen's stalls were shuttered. Lights burned and flickered behind oily window-panes. Trash and refuse of thousands of lives littered the near-ly-abandoned streets. The smell of burning wood and cooking food mingled with the fetor of filth from the street. Somewhere, someone played a merry jig on a fiddle, and voices raised in laughter and song.

Thane slipped down a side street to the stables and made his way to his gray stallion he had named Smokey. He cupped the stallion's jaw in his hand and rubbed his muzzle. "I hope you've fed well and are rested," he whispered. "Because tonight, I will need all of your strength and speed."

Smokey bobbed his head as if he understood, and Thane saddled him, making sure the girth strap was tight. Then he hurried to his lodgings, strapped on the hip quiver filled with sixty arrows and strung his powerful curved bow with its stiff tips and short limbs. It was a bow rarely found on Frei-Ock Island, but Thane had discovered that it was less cumbersome when shooting from horseback than the longbows that were more common among the Alamani. He stuffed his saddlebags with what food and water he could find. Then he adjusted the sword on his opposite hip, checked the long knife in its sheath, and whirled to leave.

He paused in the doorway and glanced back at the room that had been his home for three years. If he left now, he would become an outlaw. He wouldn't be able to remain in Coll. But Esther needed him. He couldn't betray her.

Thane mounted Smokey and kicked him toward the city gates. He kept him at a leisurely pace, though he could tell the horse was anxious to stretch his legs. He didn't need to draw attention to himself or tire the horse with a wild gallop through the city. The last of the countryfolk filed through the gates, and the guards began to drag them closed.

"One moment," Thane ordered.

The guards paused. The sergeant gazed up at him. "Sir?" he questioned.

"I am going to scout for these brigands," Thane said. "Be prepared to let me back in."

"But sir, the commander's orders were to—"

"Do not question *my* orders," Thane barked, and he kicked Smokey into a canter.

The horse's hooves pounded over the bridge. A shout rang out behind him, and Thane glanced back. Commander Cyrill stood on the battlements. Cyrill pointed, and an archer stepped up to his side. Thane didn't wait to see more. He leaned low over Smokey's neck and hissed in his ear.

Blood on the Reeds

The gray burst into a gallop, and the cool evening air swept over Thane's face. The buzz of an arrow zipped past his head. A wild thrill leapt into Thane's chest, and he smiled ruefully. He was free at last. He had snapped all the constraints that had bound him to the city away from the forest and from Esther. And yet it was a fleeting freedom. One that was destined to end in blood.

The deeper shadow of the forest enfolded Thane as Smokey galloped down the pale strip of dirt that marked the road. Cyrill clearly understood that Thane was now an outcast, and he would be coming after him. None of that mattered now. Thane had to reach the manor before it was too late.

Thane dismounted and patted Smokey's lathered neck. His own legs were stiff from the long ride.

"Rest now for a spell, my friend," he said. "We may need to run again tonight."

It had taken Thane the better part of the night to reach the manor. Now he glanced around at the smoky haze that filled the wood. The acrid reek of burning tar and roasting flesh filled the air. The flicker of the dancing flames filtered through the trees, and Thane had to suppress his desire to rush headlong into the manor. He swallowed the sickening despair and clutched at the desperate hope that the Baron of Rothe and his family had been warned, that they had time to escape.

Thane pulled the black cloak from his shoulders and draped it over Smokey's saddle. He slipped his bow from its carrying case on the saddle, and crept into the swaying shadows. The sight that met his gaze as he peered from the line of elm trees sent his blood racing.

Bodies lay in crumpled heaps in the garden—black mounds against the bright light of the flames that licked hungrily at the manor and poured gleefully from the blackened windows.

A lone figure stood atop the square tower, gazing out over the awful scene. Thane recognized him as the Baron, Esther's father. Hope leapt into this heart. He burst from the cover of the elms and raced toward the tower. If the Baron was still alive, then Esther had to be with him in the tower.

As he sped past the bodies, he realized that not all of them were

5

the Baron's retainers.

Some wore the light blue colors of the Duke of Saylen, which meant the Baron had warning.

He had tried to fight. Maybe the family had escaped.

The door to the tower sagged on its twisted hinges. Smoke billowed from the gaping, blackened hole. Several bodies sprawled over the threshold.

Thane recognized the Baron's captain of the guard, who must have fallen defending his lord. Heat washed over Thane's face, forcing him to pause at the entrance.

He peered in to find the flames devouring the beams of the ceiling overhead, but the overpowering heat drove him back. This was the only door into the keep. Thane tried again, when the beams collapsed in a roar and a shower of sparks.

He scrambled away from the burning debris that burst from the door and stood back as the flames devoured the keep. What could he do?

Stones fell from high above, and he glanced up. The Baron climbed onto one of the battlements, knocking some loose stones free. Then he spread his arms.

"Don't," Thane whispered.

The Baron swayed for a moment and fell.

"No," Thane screamed as the Baron plummeted to the ground, plunging through the clouds of smoke billowing up from his manor. His dark robe fluttered behind him as if it struggled to lift his body into the air.

The sickening crunch of flesh and bone on the cobblestone courtyard jerked the bile into Thane's throat.

He choked and coughed as he stumbled to the Baron's body.

Dark blood stained the white stones and spread out in a growing pool.

The Baron's body spasmed for a few moments before it lay still.

Thane fell to his knees, fighting the bitter tears.

He was too late.

He glanced up at the battlements on the tower, half-expecting Esther's face to appear there, but nothing moved.

Thane laid a hand on the Baron's back.

"I'm sorry," he said.

Blood on the Reeds

A whine sounded, and Thane spun around to find the great boar-hound he had trained from a puppy padding up to him. Thane had given the hound to Esther three years ago when he assumed his post at Castle Bay. The hound whimpered again, and Thane raised his hand to him. The dog nuzzled Thane's hand. He stank of singed hair. Blood caked his face and dribbled from his shoulder where a knife or sword had cut a long gash.

"Hey, old boy," Thane said. "Where is she? Where's Esther?"

The hound whined.

"Find her, boy," Thane said.

The hound whirled and bounded back toward the trees. Thane glanced once more at the Baron's body and sprang after the hound as it leapt through the corpses that lay scattered around the burning manor and into the copse of beeches and maples behind it.

They followed the line of silent corpses belonging to the house-hold servants who had died as they rushed to escape the manor. When they reached the clearing where the Baron had held the mid-summer feast for all of his retainers, Thane paused. He caught the cry of shock and dismay that nearly escaped his lips. On the far side of the clearing, Esther and Thane's own mother sagged against the ropes that bound them to two large maple trees. All around them lay the bodies of the Baron's household servants. It hadn't been a battle. It had been a massacre.

Heedless of the danger, Thane burst from the cover of the trees and raced across the clearing. His despair grew when he noted the feathered shafts of half a dozen arrows protruding from each of their bodies. The horror of it caught the breath in his throat. He dropped his bow, whipped his knife from its sheath, and cut them both down. He lay them gently on the trampled, bloody grass and fell to his knees beside them.

His mother's eyes were opened wide in an unblinking stare of death. The once playful animation of her features had frozen in a grimace of pain. A dribble of blood stained her pale, white cheek. Thane coughed on the sob and worked his jaw, struggling to keep his emotions in check. Why his mother? She hadn't done anything. It hadn't occurred to him that they might murder his mother.

Esther groaned and stirred. Her eyes fluttered open. Thane lifted her hand. It was deathly cold. He glanced at the arrows that had

7

punctured her body. All but one were non-lethal wounds, as if the murderers had wanted to inflict pain yet keep her alive. One arrow had penetrated her right breast. It would have missed the heart, but it had certainly punctured a lung. Esther would be drowning in her own blood. The hound nudged her cheek with his nose as if he wanted her to get up.

"I knew you'd come," she choked.

"I'm sorry," Thane said. "I should have been here."

She squeezed his hand feebly. "It doesn't matter," she said. "You have to leave now. They're waiting for you."

Thane scowled and looked around. In his rush, he hadn't seen any sign of the Duke's men.

"I love you," Esther said. The shadow of a smile touched her beautiful lips.

Thane brushed a lock of brown hair from before her eyes. His lips trembled. His chest burned. He would give anything to have been here to protect her. But the Baron had insisted that he elevate himself before he would let him marry his daughter. That was why Thane had gone to the city.

"I know," he said. "I love you, too."

"I would have waited for you until the end," she said.

Thane bent and kissed her forehead when the quiet thrum of a bowstring sounded. He jerked upright as an arrow narrowly missed him and slapped into Esther's side. She grunted. Her gaze found his, and he watched as the light faded from her eyes. She let out a final quiet sigh.

Thane stared in dismay. She was gone. He couldn't believe that she was gone. His whole world lay in ruin.

Another arrow whipped past his head.

The hound snarled.

Thane grabbed up his bow and leapt behind the huge maple as a line of men-at-arms broke from the cover of the trees and stepped into the clearing.

Others crashed through the trees behind him.

Thane was trapped.

Rage roared in his chest. He ground his teeth.

They had left him nothing to live for. He would sell his life dearly.

"Captain!"

Blood on the Reeds

A harsh whisper sounded behind him.

Thane spun to find a boy crouching in the huckleberry bushes. It was Owen, the boy who visited the Baron every summer. His family were minor nobles from the southern Oban Plain.

Owen gestured to him. "This way," he said.

Frowning, Thane glanced back at the closing circle of men and then at Esther and his mother. There was nothing he could do for them now, but the boy was still alive.

Thane reluctantly slipped into the underbrush. They had covered only a dozen yards when Owen cried out in surprise.

A dark shadow loomed over him.

Thane nocked an arrow, drew, and loosed.

The shadow staggered and groaned.

More shadows joined him, and Thane loosed two more times.

In the thrashing and chaos that erupted around them, he, Owen, and the hound slipped past the circle of men through the gap Thane's arrows had created.

Thane led Owen to where he had left his big gray horse.

He threw the cloak aside, leapt into the saddle, and dragged Owen up in front of him.

Smokey shied at the sight and smell of the hound, but Thane kicked him into a gallop out of the manor grounds and onto the road. The sounds of the chase filled the woods around them. Smokey strode forward, but Thane could feel the horse's exhaustion. He was already tired from the long ride. They wouldn't get far with fresh horses on their tail. Thane's only hope was to shake their pursuers or make it to too costly for them to follow.

Smokey pounded around a bend in the road with the hound loping beside him, when moonlight glinted off the helmets and spears of a troop of men holding the road in front of him. Thane checked Smokey and reined him to the left down a narrow track barely visible in the darkness.

The trail snaked its way through the woods toward the river. Thane pushed Owen down and bent over the boy to avoid low-hanging branches. Smokey's hooves clicked against the stones and stumbled over roots until they broke from the trees and clambered down the last rise before the river.

Smokey slipped and went down.

Thane jerked Owen from the saddle and kicked free of the stirrups.

He landed hard, trying to scramble away from the thrashing hooves, but one caught him in the back and sent him flying headlong onto the stony ground.

The air burst from his lungs.

He groveled on the ground, struggling for breath, as Smokey righted himself and limped a few paces before he stood, sides heaving and trembling.

Smokey was blown and lame.

Thane stayed on his hands and knees until his breath returned and then glanced at Owen.

The boy stood beside a maple, watching him with eyes that said he understood their predicament. He knew they were about to die.

Thane's lungs finally expanded, and he rose to his feet, sucking in the rich air of the forest. He glanced at Smokey and whispered a curse. Thane snatched up his bow and checked it for damage. He strode to Smokey's side to grab the extra quiver of arrows and the saddlebags before slapping the horse on the rump.

Smokey jogged a few steps and then stopped. He looked back at Thane as if to ask whether or not he were coming.

"Go," Thane order with a wave of his hand. Smokey bobbed his head. "Go," he said again, and the horse limped down the trail.

Thane watched him go with a sinking feeling in the pit of his stomach. Without a horse, they would never escape. But a lame horse was worse than useless.

"Follow me," Thane whispered to Owen.

They pushed into the canebrake with the hound following close behind. Thane had spent his youth playing, hunting, and fishing along this river. He knew the area well. The problem was getting out with a host of men hunting him. The river flowed deep and swift here amid a jumble of boulders that made crossing impossible. The nearest ford was more than a mile upstream. The canebrake hugged the riverbank for a good mile, and it was at least a hundred yards wide—sometimes more, depending on the lay of the land. The canes grew as tall as a man. They were as thick as his finger and clustered close together.

Thane stumbled onto a narrow game trail and followed it deep into the canebrake. He was searching for the rise where the cane thinned. When he found it, Thane pulled Owen down beside him and raised a finger to his lips. He drew his boot knife and handed it to Owen.

"Don't make a sound," he whispered. "I'll be back."

He pointed at the hound. "Stay," he ordered.

The hound whined and then sat on his haunches. Thane crept away into the reeds. He would prepare a few surprises for any who followed them.

The gray dawn found Thane and Owen huddled on the rise deep in the canebrake with the hound sprawled at their feet. A breeze rustled the cane, making it sigh like a dying animal. It brought with it the fresh smell of the river and the promise of rain. Owen knelt before a line of a dozen sticks arranged in a fan in front of him. Each one had a string tied to it that trailed off into the canebrake. It was the best Thane could do. He hoped it would be enough.

The clip of hooves on stone and the jangle of harnesses carried on the breeze. The soldiers were searching the trail. Thane studied Owen now by the light of day as he waited for the struggle to begin. It wouldn't be long once the soldiers discovered where Smokey had gone down.

Owen's lips pinched tight. His face was streaked with soot and blood. He couldn't be more than nine or ten years old, but he was tall for his age and quick to understand. Owen's fine, blonde hair camouflaged nicely with the reeds. Thane knew that Owen would be killed if he were found here. They wouldn't want to leave any witnesses—not when the traitors would want to justify their coup and assert their right to rule.

Uncomfortable things, like little boys who tell the truth, would need to be eliminated. Still, Thane couldn't see a way to get the boy out. The lands Owen's father held were far to the south and east. Without a horse and hunted as they were, they would never make it that far.

The mist rose off the waters of the Spey River. It lifted in spiraling columns to join the clouds that drifted into the trees and grasses along the bank. Thane had spent many mornings in the skiff out on the gently rolling river below the rapids fishing for trout and bass. The quiet peace of the scene brought the sting of tears to his eyes and an overwhelming sense of loss and grief.

He had come so far from those days of poverty and obscurity, and now those were the days he longed for—the days when he and Esther could steal away for a few hours to wander the woodland trails and soak their feet in the murmuring river—the days when he and his mother lived in the little cabin behind the manor, alone and secure in the affection they shared. Those were the days before the Baron had sent him away—before he had been discovered by the King who honored him and made him a man-at-arms.

The sweet days of youth had vanished to be replaced by this—hiding like a vagabond amid the reeds where he used to play, awaiting certain death, while his mother's and Esther's blood soaked into the leafy forest floor. And for what? So a power-hungry noble could seize the throne.

Thane's only crime was that he had been loyal to the King. Esther had been murdered because Hassani blood flowed in her veins. And his mother simply because she was his mother. The Duke of Saylen had betrayed his own family for an upstart noble named Geric. Thane had met Geric once and knew him to be a hard, calculating man. Geric would remember Thane's loyalties. He would never let Thane go free.

Thane watched as a blackbird landed on a reed, causing it to sway and bend under its weight. He gave a rueful smile. He was swaying and bending under the weight of the tragedy unfolding around him, but he wouldn't break—not yet. Still, if he could have chosen his place to die, this would be it. Here, amid the precious memories of youth.

The soft thud of horse's hooves on the damp, leaf-covered ground paused, followed by the rustle of canes. Thane gazed up at the gray sky and black clouds that rolled in on the growing breeze. Then he glanced over at Owen and nodded. He pointed to the sticks he had arranged before them.

"Start with the one on the right," he said. "Wait for my whistle."

He rose to leave, then turned to face Owen once again.

"If I don't come back," he said, "take to the river. There's a ford a few miles up where you can cross and seek the western road."

Blood on the Reeds

Owen nodded but remained silent. The grim expression on his face told Thane that Owen fully expected to die. Thane grasped his bow and slipped down the trail to a gap in the reeds where the canes thinned enough to give him room to shoot. He positioned himself on the boulder to wait. The rustle of the canes grew louder. Thane nocked an arrow and whistled. The canes in front of him jerked.

"There," someone shouted.

The shapes of skulking soldiers appeared in the reeds.

Thane drew and loosed.

The soldier cried out.

Others rushed to his aid.

Thane shot three more before slipping away to the next ambush.

He whistled again, the reeds jerked, and a cry went up as the soldiers worked their way toward the new sounds of rustling reeds.

Thane waited until they were in view and shot two more in rapid succession before slipping away again.

This cat and mouse game continued as Owen kept tugging at the strings in response to Thane's whistles. The sun climbed steadily higher into the overcast sky, and the cool of the morning gave way to the moist heat of early afternoon. The soldiers had stopped taking the bait, and Thane waited to see what they would do, when the smell of smoke reached him.

They were burning the canebrake.

Thane scrambled back to where Owen crouched, holding another stick in his hands. Thane grabbed the stick and gave the string several more jerks before he seized Owen and pointed him toward the river. Thane threw the saddlebags over his shoulder as the smoke billowed above the canes and rolled through the canebrake. He hustled Owen down the sloping hill to the rock overhang that would give them cover. The canes were dry this time of year, and they would burn fast and hot.

They crawled down the game trail with the hound behind them to the marshy part of the brake where the water soaked their trousers and squeezed between their fingers from the thick, green moss. The sounds of crackling fire and the roiling clouds of smoke pursued them. The heat of the fire warmed Thane's back, and the smoke rolled through the brake, making it hard to breathe.

When they reached the pile of boulders that pushed out over the

13

river, Thane slid down the muddy bank to splash into the water up to his knees.

The murmur of the rapids dampened the sounds of the crackling fire behind them. The cold water felt refreshing after the stifling heat of the canebrake. Thane ducked under the rock overhang and froze.

An old man crouched against the boulder, covered in mud and grime and clothed in the brown colors of the Baron's household. Blood caked the side of his gray head, but Thane recognized him as the Baron's old armorer.

Thane opened his mouth to speak, but the old man raised a finger to his lips. Thane crawled over to him, trying to keep his bow dry. Owen slipped in behind him with a quiet splash. The hound stood behind Owen in water up to his chest, lapping at the river.

The old armorer's gaze rested on Owen. His expression darkened, and he pointed up the river.

"I'll distract them," he whispered.

Thane shook his head. The old man gestured to Owen.

"The boy should live," he breathed.

He splashed past them and scrambled up the muddy bank. Thane reached out to stop him but hesitated. The old man had a right to choose his time to die. Thane would not dishonor it by throwing away his sacrifice.

"Let's go," he said to Owen.

They waded upriver, slipping in the muddy bottom and stumbling over stones until they reached the edge of the rock overhang. Thane crawled on his belly to peer over the bank. A flash of blue told him the soldiers had circled around, expecting to flush them out with the fire in the reeds. Thane nocked an arrow, raised up on one knee, and drew, when a cry broke out. The soldier hiding in the reeds jerked and spun away to sprint back down the river. They must have found the old man.

Thane motioned for Owen to come, and together they raced through the reeds towards the stand of maple and beech beyond. The hound padded along behind them.

They broke from the reeds and sprinted across the open ground for the cover of the trees when something slammed into the side of Thane's knee.

Pain lanced through his leg, and his knee buckled.

Blood on the Reeds

He fell, sprawling headlong onto the stones.

Then he scrambled to one knee and glanced down in rising panic at the feathered shaft that protruded from the side of his other knee.

A bowstring slapped, and Thane lunged sideways as another arrow zipped past, cutting through his tunic and slicing a long gash in his side. Thane scrambled behind the nearest beech and waved for Owen to take cover, but the boy was already crouching behind a fallen maple. Thane jerked an arrow from his quiver and nocked it, searching for the hidden archer. He hissed to the hound.

"Sic 'em, boy," he commanded.

The hound wagged its tail and darted into the reeds.

Thane leaned against the cool, smooth bark of the beech. The old armorer's words came back to him. "The boy should live." It didn't matter what happened to Thane now. He had nothing to live for. But Owen still had his entire life ahead of him, and he could be a witness to the Duke's betrayal.

The hound's growl rumbled through the thickening haze. There was a flash of movement on the edge of the wood, and Thane drew and loosed. A shriek rang out and was cut off by a horrible gurgling and growling. The hound came into view, dragging the kicking, writhing man by his throat. Thane swallowed against the disgust that choked him. That was no way for a man to die. The hound jerked his head back and forth with a growl, and Thane looked away. He gestured for Owen to go.

"Run," he whispered.

Owen shook his head.

"There's no time," Thane said. Why couldn't the boy understand?

Owen rose to his feet and crossed the distance between them in four quick strides. He grabbed Thane's arm and tried to drag him to his feet. Thane resisted and then gave in. He pulled himself up. The arrow embedded in his knee scraped at the movement, sending excruciating pain coursing through him. Nausea rose in his throat. He cursed and yanked on the arrow. The shaft came free, but the point remained embedded in the bone.

Owen lifted Thane's arm around his shoulders, and they hobbled into the shadows of the maples and beeches. The hound padded up to them with fresh blood dripping from his chin, his tail wagging.

Thane allowed Owen to struggle on with him until they reached a grassy hillock that overlooked the bend in the river. At the base of the hill, a pile of boulders overgrown with witch hazel and mint crowded next to the river. A few boulders had spilled into the water, creating a little eddy. Thane paused and then continued to the boulders where he sat down and tried to stretch his leg. It was becoming stiff—almost too stiff to move. The blood from the wound in his side had already clotted—but not before it had soaked his shirt. His limbs trembled, and the dizziness made him blink and clutch at the large stone for stability.

Thane drained his waterskin and handed it to Owen to refill at the river. He waited until Owen was bent over the water, braced himself, and grabbed the end of the point that protruded from his knee. It was slippery with blood, but he worked it back and forth and up and down, trying to free it from the bone.

He gasped and trembled. Sweat dripped from his brow. Gritting his teeth against the pain, he kept at it until the point came free with a jerk. The flash of agony sent the nausea burning through his stomach and up into his chest. For a moment, he thought he would throw up, but he coughed and kept it down.

He fell against the cool stone and closed his eyes. When he opened them, Owen stood over him, his lips pinched tight in a frown. Thane held up the bloody point, and Owen bent to help him tie a strip of cloth around the injured knee. When he finished, Thane placed a hand on Owen's shoulder.

"You have to go on, lad," he said.

Owen shook his head. "I can't. I can't leave you like this."

"Take the dog," Thane said.

He fumbled with his sword belt until it slipped free, and he handed it to Owen. Owen hesitated, then took it.

"There's a ford another hundred yards upriver," Thane said. "Cross and follow the river for several miles until you reach an old stone monument where a path comes out of the woods. The path will take you to the west road and your father's lands."

"Come with me," Owen said.

Thane understood the boy's fear, but it couldn't be helped. Not now.

"I can't," Thane said, gesturing to his leg. "I'll delay them while you get away."

Blood on the Reeds

A determined, rebellious expression crept over Owen's face. His frown deepened.

"I'm not a coward," he said.

Thane permitted a smile. Youth always saw things in such black and white. They always thought life was so simple. So easy.

"There's no point in both of us dying," Thane said.

"They said they were supposed to kill you," Owen said. "I heard them talking. They said you would come as soon as you heard. One man said it wasn't right and the lords should just kill each other and leave the rest of us out of it. But another said he should keep his mouth shut and be glad he wasn't you. He said Geric had sent special orders that you were to be killed and your head brought to Chullish as proof."

Thane studied Owen. He wasn't surprised to learn that Geric had been thorough in his instructions. But no boy Owen's age should have to confront the cruelty of the world like this—not yet. Thane picked a leaf of mint and crushed it between his fingers. He lifted it to his nose to inhale the fresh aroma.

"I'm sorry," Thane said. "The only thing I can do now is see that you, at least, survive this massacre."

Owen shook his head again.

"Now listen carefully to me, Owen," Thane said as he placed a bloody hand on Owen's shoulder. "I know you're scared, and I know you have a long, frightening journey ahead of you. But you have to be brave. Your family will be allowed to live because you aren't directly related to the Hassani. So, I'm entrusting my sword to you. This sword has never been raised in an evil deed. And it has only ever been drawn in defense of the true kings of Coll. Do you understand?

"Yes," Owen said.

"Good. I want you to keep it safe until the time is right. I pray that some Hassani will find a way to survive and come back for his throne. You must be ready when he does. Then I expect you to avenge me and Esther and all the others who have been murdered here. Can you do that for me, Owen?"

Owen frowned. "Okay," he said. Tears welled up in his eyes, but he kept them in.

"That's a good lad," Thane said. He handed Owen the saddlebags.

"Good luck, son. May the ancients guide your footsteps." This was the phrase Thane's mother used every time he left the cabin. "Now go, before they find us."

Owen hesitated, then draped the saddlebags over his shoulder. Thane patted the hound and pointed to Owen. "Heel," he said. The hound hesitated, confused. "Heel," he said again as he gestured for Owen to leave. Owen turned. The hound whined and nuzzled Thane's hand.

"Thank you, old boy," he said. "Now, heel."

The hound trotted after Owen and then glanced back. Thane snapped his fingers. "Heel," he commanded. The hound followed Owen.

"Stay with him, boy," Thane whispered as he watched Owen and the dog slip amid the boulders to disappear among the tall meadow grasses and willows that hugged the riverbank. He swallowed the knot in his throat as the quiet of the hillside pressed in upon him. Even though Owen was just a boy, his presence had helped keep the despair at bay. Now Thane was alone and seriously injured. It was only a matter of time.

Thane grabbed a handful of mint leaves and stuffed them in his mouth. The burst of fresh mint drove away the edge off weariness that burned his eyes. He shifted and winced at the tightness in his back where Smokey had kicked him and the leg that was swelling fast from the arrow wound. He wouldn't get far if he tried to move, but he still had forty good arrows and a long, open, sloping hill before him.

Thane rose and, using the stones for balance, hopped to the upper edge of the pile of boulders where he could command a view of the hillside and the riverbank. The reeds and meadow grasses came closer to the boulders than he would have liked, but he could still spy anyone approaching from that direction.

He settled on a boulder and stretched his leg. The knee was so swollen now that it pushed tight against his trousers and the bandage Owen had applied. He could barely move it, but that didn't matter now. He needed to delay them long enough to give Owen a head start. Besides, they had come for *his* head—not Owen's. If he offered himself to them, they might let the boy alone.

Thane slipped an arrow from his hip quiver and nocked it. Some-

Blood on the Reeds

how, knowing that he was about to die gave him a sense of calm he hadn't experienced in a long time. He gazed out over the gently flowing river where a ray of late afternoon light cut through the overcast sky to dance on its surface. The cattails and meadow grasses bowed to the gentle breeze. A blue heron lifted itself from the bank and rose into the air.

A great hush settled over the land, as if it knew that a man who loved it was about to die. As if it knew the blood of innocent men, women, and children even now soaked into its soil. As if it knew Thane's blood was about to join theirs.

More than an hour later, the jangle of a bridle sounded faintly on the breeze with the occasional creak of leather. They were coming. The land waited in silence. Even the finches and warblers had gone quiet.

A lone man on foot appeared in the shadows of the beeches and maples. He surveyed the hillside with its pile of boulders for a moment before he bent to study the ground. Then he rose to discuss something with someone behind him. The men spread out along the line of trees, being careful to use them for cover. Thane gave the scout grudging respect. He anticipated a possible ambush and was taking precautions. Well, they wouldn't be disappointed.

The line advanced cautiously down the hill.

Thane waited until the men were within easy range before he drew the string to his ear, let out his breath slowly, and released.

He jerked another arrow from his quiver, drew, and released again.

A cry rose up as the first arrow found its mark.

Two more men fell before someone shouted and pointed to where Thane nestled among the rocks and underbrush, breathing in the fresh scent of mint.

The men closest to him rushed.

Thane managed two more shots before they were too close.

He dropped his bow and jerked the long hunting knife from its sheath.

As the men reached him, an arrow punched into his hip, sending lightning pains shooting down his leg.

Thane flailed at the sword stroke, barely managing to deflect it.

He swept his knife across the man's belly.

"Hold!"

A great voice boomed over the hillside and echoed off the boulders.

The men hesitated and stepped back.

Thane leaned heavily on the rough stone and dragged his sleeve across his face to wipe the sweat from his eyes. His hands trembled. He blinked at the rising nausea and searing pain.

A man wearing a blue surcoat over a mail shirt rode down the hill on a great buckskin stallion.

It was the Duke of Saylen.

The Duke was only a few years older than Thane, in his mid-twenties, but already he had a reputation as a skilled warrior and talented military leader. Thane had served him for over three years before he had joined the King's army. The Duke was a stout young man with short-cropped, sandy-brown hair, and dark eyes. He reined his horse to a stop and looked down on Thane as the man Thane had injured crawled away to be helped by his friends.

"Stand several paces back," the Duke ordered.

"My Lord?" one of the men questioned.

"Do it," the Duke shouted, and the men retreated.

The Duke dismounted and stood holding the buckskin's reins loosely in his hands. He studied Thane as if deciding on something.

Thane sneered at him. Here was the man that had betrayed his King and his family. The man who had ordered the slaughter of innocent women and children. Thane raised the bloody knife he still clutched in his hand.

The Duke stepped toward him until he was only a couple of paces away, but he might as well have been a mile away. Thane couldn't even stumble two steps to punish the man that had permitted all of this suffering.

"I'm sorry," the Duke whispered.

At first, Thane thought he had misunderstood him. Then he stared in confusion. He had expected anything but this.

"I did what I had to do," the Duke said.

"You're a traitor and a murderer," Thane snarled.

An expression of bitter sadness swept over the Duke's face, and he bowed his head to mask it.

"You're right," he said, "but try to understand—"

"No," Thane shouted.

Blood on the Reeds

The Duke's head snapped up and his hand reached for the pommel of his sword.

"Come here and let me kill you as you deserve," Thane growled. "Then they can take both our heads as presents for Geric, the butcher."

The Duke's brow furrowed. "I will not be taking your head," he said in a low voice that didn't carry. "I want you to join me. I need people who are still loyal. I can protect you."

Thane scoffed. "You expect me to believe that?"

The Duke shrugged. "Heads can be disfigured," he said. "And you have given us plenty to choose from."

Thane stared in disbelief. What was the Duke saying?

"You're gravely injured," the Duke said. "Let me help you."

The Duke reached a hand toward Thane and stepped forward.

Thane raised the knife with a snarl of rage.

Something hissed and slammed into his armpit, biting deep.

Thane gasped. The knife fell from his numb fingers. He slumped against the stone as the Duke rushed to support him.

"Hold!" the Duke yelled. "I said hold!"

Thane blinked and sucked in short, shallow breaths against the fire that burned in his chest.

The Duke's lips pinched tight, and his brow furrowed in apparent concern.

A snarl echoed amid the boulders, and the great hound came bounding toward him.

The Duke jumped back to avoid the snap of the hound's jaws.

Thane blinked. The hound shouldn't be here. He should be with Owen. Thane raised his head to peer out over the river and found the slight form of the boy standing next to a witch hazel tree with the saddlebags still over his shoulder, watching him.

Despair filled Thane's heart. Not Owen. The foolish boy should have run. He glanced at the hound who stood between him and the Duke with water dripping from his fur. The hound's lips lifted in a snarl.

The Duke raised his hand to keep his men back. A look of pity swept over his face.

"I'm sorry," he said again. "I would have protected you."

Thane's breathing stuttered. He blinked rapidly, trying to clear the

21

haze from before his eyes.

"Esther," he mumbled. "You killed Esther."

The Duke bowed his head and turned away. He mounted his horse. Some men stepped forward, but the hound snarled a warning.

"Leave him," the Duke ordered. The Duke gazed out over the river to where Owen stood.

"Please," Thane gasped. "Not the boy, please."

The Duke studied him and then nodded.

Thane couldn't keep his feet any longer. He slumped against the stone and slid to the ground. The hound whined and licked his face. Thane raised a hand to pat him as the world closed in around him. The smell of crushed mint and wet dog filled his nostrils. A ringing sounded in his ears. Esther's face filled his vision. She beckoned to him. Thane let out one last ragged sigh and drifted into the darkness.

Tears slipped down Owen's cheeks to drip from his chin. Thane no longer moved, and the men withdrew up the hill. Owen was all alone again. The Duke had looked right at him and still turned away. Owen waited until the men had disappeared into the trees before racing back to the ford to splash his way across the river. By the time he reached the boulders, a steady drizzle fell from the gray skies.

When Owen burst through the undergrowth, Thane was gone. Hope swelled in Owen's chest until his gaze followed the bloody trail that smeared the grass up to the summit of the hillock where Thane's body now lay. The great hound sat on his haunches beside Thane. Owen scrambled up the hill, but, when he approached Thane's body, the hound growled. Owen stopped.

"It's okay, boy," he said.

He gazed at the dog in confusion. Why had the hound dragged Thane's body all the way up here? Owen fell to his knees and reached a hand out to touch Thane's shoulder. The hound growled again, but Owen ignored him. He slipped the sword belt over his head, laid the sword on Thane's chest, and lifted his hand to the pommel.

The hound threw back his head and let out a mournful howl that rang over the trees. And he kept howling as if he wanted the world to know that his master was slain and that he mourned his loss.

The sound brought the knot into this Owen's throat and the tears

Blood on the Reeds

to his eyes. Owen bowed his head, trying to forget all the horror he had seen. He didn't understand any of it. The exhaustion he had been fighting for so long pressed upon him, and he fell in the grass as the sobs escaped his throat.

Owen awoke to the stomp of horses' hooves and a snarl. He jerked to a sitting position and found the Duke peering down at him. Owen glanced around for the other soldiers, but only three sat on their horses behind the Duke. The hound held his ground with his hackles raised, but the Duke didn't try to approach.

"He's gone," the Duke said. "Let us take you home."

Owen grabbed Thane's sword and dragged it from the sheath. It was heavy, but he hefted it and rose to his feet. He would protect Thane's body, if he could.

"There's no need for that," the Duke said. "We aren't here to harm you."

Owen's mind raced. The Duke was the traitor. Maybe now was his chance to avenge Thane and Esther and the rest of those who had died. He stepped toward the Duke, but the Duke shook his head.

"Put the sword away, lad, before you hurt yourself."

He gestured to one of the men, who dismounted, but the man stopped when the hound bounded toward him. The horses shied.

"You saw that I tried to save him," the Duke said. "I didn't order any of this. This is all Geric's doing. If you come away with us now, I can get you safely home before anyone even knows you were here."

Owen lowered the sword. He glanced at the hound and then at Thane.

"Are you going to kill the hound?" he asked.

The Duke shook his head. "I wouldn't dream of it," he said. "A loyal dog like that should be honored, not killed. I'm leaving two men here to guard Thane's body and his faithful hound. When the dog lets them, they'll bury him here on the hill where his hound wanted him to rest."

Owen glanced at the man who had dismounted.

The Duke gestured to him. "Liam will escort you home," he said.

Owen puckered his brow. He didn't know what to do. The hound whined, apparently satisfied the men meant his master no harm. He padded around Thane's body, lay down beside him, and rested his head on Thane's chest to blink up at the Duke.

Owen sheathed the sword. He would have to wait for another day to avenge Thane and the others who had died. He would wait until the true king returned.

AUTHOR'S NOTE

The inspiration for Thane's character came from my reading of Japanese history. A famous Samurai learned that his master had been murdered and that his master's enemies were coming after him. He fled to his family's lands only to find the emperor's forces waiting for him.

He escaped into the reeds along the river and employed the ingenious strategy of using strings tied to reeds to misdirect the enemy and guide them into the open where he could shoot them with his longbow. His skill and courage were unparalleled, but he was still trapped. There was no way out of the reeds. After he was injured in the knee by an arrow, he threw his sword into the river so that this enemies could not obtain it, drew his knife, and stabbed himself in the throat.

When his enemies came to get his body, his faithful hound drove them off, and, when they proposed to shoot the hound, the emperor forbade it on the grounds that the loyalty and bravery shown by the archer and his hound should be honored. The hound then dragged his master's body up to a hill and laid down to die beside him. The emperor ordered a monument to be erected to honor the brave samurai and his faithful dog.

I used the story to explore the consequences of the Duke of Saylen's betrayal of his family and to show that, from the beginning, he was working to gather loyal subjects who survived the blood bath in an attempt to undercut Geric's power. Owen was caught in the middle of the coup as a young boy, and his short, traumatic experience with Thane made him one of the most ardent and loyal servants of the Hassani royal family. He proved so trustworthy and capable that Brion selected him to manage his ducal estates while Brion and Finola went in search of Brion's mother.

THE HIDDEN ARCHER

Death floated on the breeze. Redmond reined in his horse and squinted up at the ravens that circled above the heathland as they descended in ever-narrowing spirals. He glanced at Aengus, who rode up beside him.

The warm August wind rustled the heather and kicked up lazy cyclones of dust. The repulsively sweet aroma of spoiled fruit mixed with feces and rotten eggs wafted over the rise in front of them. Death always smelled like this. There were certainly bodies over that rise, and they had been cooking in the summer sun for some time.

Redmond kicked free of the stirrups and slid from the saddle. Though ravens might not only flock to battlefields, the stench of death could not be ignored. Redmond suppressed the tremor of fear that rippled through his stomach. He had been following his brother's scouting party. Those circling crows and the smell of death suggested an ambush, and the lay of the land provided ample opportunity for one.

The rolling heathland spread out from the Laro Forest to the south and east. Deep gullies, cut by gurgling creeks, sliced eastward to join the Skye River. Rocky crags and broken ravines funneled travelers north along predictable trails. Neahl's path led up and over the rise in front of them between two great boulders where the short grass and the heather had been trampled by their passing. The ravens dipped and soared overhead.

Redmond wiped the sweat from his forehead with his sleeve. He glanced up at Aengus, expecting him to dismount as well, but the burly young man from the southern Taber Wood didn't seem to understand the meaning of the circling ravens or notice the smell of death. Redmond was too used to riding with Neahl and Weyland. They always understood the signs and respected them.

26

The Hidden Archer

"Best check it out," Redmond said.

He slipped the quiver from his back, withdrew four arrows with broadheads from his quiver, and hefted his longbow. He had no intention of riding headlong into danger.

Redmond and Aengus had ridden through the night to bring Neahl word that the Salassani were circling around behind them and would soon cut them off from King Geric's armies in Laro Forest. A big battle was coming, and the King wanted Neahl and his men back with the rest of the army.

The ravens might mean that Neahl had been caught unawares—that Redmond had arrived too late. He tried not to consider the worst, but the sick feeling in his gut wouldn't go away. Neahl might be on the other side of that hill, dead or dying. Redmond couldn't imagine a world without his big brother in it.

Neahl's presence had dominated Redmond's life from his earliest memories—and not just because Neahl was a big, imposing man. Neahl was brave and daring, strong and true. Neahl had come for him after the Salassani raid had destroyed their village. Neahl had single-handedly tracked the Salassani who had killed his young bride and shot them all before being captured himself.

The Salassani had tortured him and severed the fingers from his right hand so he could no longer draw a bow. But Neahl had persisted, and now he was a captain of the King's scouts who had dedicated his life to hunting Salassani wherever he could find them. Redmond had followed him. He would follow him to the grave, despite the warnings of his own bride-to-be, Lara. He had no other choice. Neahl was the only family he had left. It was his duty.

Aengus grunted and dropped from his saddle. "You're overly cautious," he said.

Redmond scowled at him. Aengus was a few inches taller than Redmond and more burly, though more than one man had come to regret underestimating Redmond's wiry frame.

"You don't smell it?" Redmond asked.

Aengus raised his nose to the breeze. "It just smells like sulfur," he said.

Redmond grunted in disgust, adjusted his leather armguard, and made sure his shooting glove was comfortable. How many men had been led to their deaths because they couldn't recognize the smell of danger? Redmond had known Salassani who could smell the urine of an animal from thirty paces and tell you what kind it was.

In moments like these, that kind of skill and the caution born of experience were the only things likely to keep a man alive. Headstrong men, overconfident in their own prowess, usually ended up crumpled amid the heather, their life's blood leaching into the parched earth. Redmond had seen it many times before.

They left the horses by the great boulders to graze on the dry grasses and skulked up the hillside on hands and knees under the burning sun. There was precious little cover in the rocky ravine. Purple and white heather scattered amid the bunches of grass and low scrub. Even on their hands and knees, the men stood out. Aengus's light brown hair contrasted with the white heather, and his bulk made him look like a deformed bull crawling through the grass.

Redmond squirmed the last dozen paces to the top of the hill on his belly, like a snake in the dirt. He tasted the sharp flavor of the heather as he paused below the rise. He clasped his bow and the four arrows he brought with him in one hand. Aengus had followed his example, though he did not carry a bow. They both had short swords strapped to their waists, and Redmond's sheathed knives pressed uncomfortably into his body as he dragged himself through the brush.

A flutter of wings and the caws of the ravens told Redmond that someone or something was alive on the other side of the ridge. It could be a coyote or a wolf nosing around the corpses. It could be a survivor, still clinging to life. But it might be an impatient Salassani lying in ambush. Redmond wiggled up behind a bunch of heather and peered over the rise.

A green valley spread out before him. It was surrounded on three sides by crumbling boulders and gnarled old junipers. A broad trail cut through the center to disappear around a bend at the far end. In the center, a puddle of water glistened in the August sun. A copse of trees enfolded a tangle of boulders on one side of the vale. Halfway to the pond, a small pile of stones no higher than a man's knee and as long as four men stretched head to toe had been left as a cairn by travelers. There was no other cover in the vale—just the usual scrub heather and low grasses.

Redmond had guessed right. The brutal remains of an ambush scattered about the valley. Several riderless horses wandered about,

The Hidden Archer

nibbling at the grass or drinking from the puddle. A dozen men stretched out in death—some Salassani, but most Alamani. Even from the cover of the hill, the ghastly wounds and the lifeless faces of men he knew were visible. One man tried to crawl toward the water. Another swatted at the ravens that hopped around him. None of the rest stirred. Redmond forced himself to remain calm as he searched the vale and the surrounding rocks carefully for any sign of Neahl or of any remaining Salassani warriors.

"By the Gods," Aengus whispered. "That's Davin. My brother, Davin."

Aengus tried to lunge to his feet, but Redmond placed a hand on his back and shoved him down to the dirt.

"Do you want to die?" he asked.

"Get your hand off me," Aengus demanded. "There's no one here." He rose to his feet and loped down the hill.

"The idiot," Redmond said. He heard the hiss of the arrow before it passed in front of Aengus. The shaft barely missed Aengus's head. Aengus lurched to a stop. Redmond realized that even on the hillside he was exposed.

"Down you fool," Redmond cried as he sprinted after Aengus and launched himself behind the long pile of stones. Aengus dove to the ground as another arrow grazed his head. He scrambled on hands and knees to collapse beside Redmond behind the stone pile.

"Where is he?" Aengus said. "The Salassani filth."

"Don't know," Redmond said. "By the direction of the shot, I'd guess he was by that bunch of junipers."

Aengus craned his neck to peer over the rocks.

"Let's rush him," he said. "He can't shoot us both."

Redmond stared at him. Why were southerners so stupid when it came to the Salassani?

"If he's any kind of archer at all," Redmond said, "he'll have five or six arrows in the air before we can even reach the first boulder."

Aengus clicked his tongue in disgust. He craned his neck around again. "I can't see him."

"You won't," Redmond said. Neahl had beaten this lesson into him from the very start of his training.

"Always remember," Neahl said, "that social animals and humans almost always leave a lookout."

29

"Animals?" Redmond asked.

Neahl rubbed his eyes and passed a hand over the stubble on his chin.

"Yes, animals," he said. "I once watched a wolf pack work its way across the heather. They had scouts out front—flankers—and even a large she-wolf that stayed behind to keep an eye on an injured wolf that couldn't keep up with the rest. The Salassani never leave a camp unguarded or unwatched. Even if you can't see him, the lookout is there."

"How do you find them?" Redmond asked.

"You look," Neahl said.

Redmond grimaced. "That much I figured out on my own. I meant what do the Salassani do to conceal themselves when they're on watch?"

"They choose the high ground," Neahl said, "so they can see in all directions, but they stay low and in the shadows. You won't see them until they move, and they're very good at holding still. They're trained to do it from a young age."

Redmond frowned. "What if their first move is to draw and release?" he asked. "Then it's too late."

"That's why you have to see them first." Neahl smiled.

Redmond scowled. "Nice. The only way I know that I saw them first is that I don't have an arrow in my belly."

"That's about the size of it," Neahl said.

The memory made Redmond smile.

"You think this is funny?" Aengus demanded. Sweat dripped from his brow and mixed with the blood leaking from the gash caused by the arrow. The bloody sweat left streaks on his face. His dull-brown tunic and green trousers were covered in dust.

"I think you might as well relax," Redmond said, "because we're going to be here until dark."

Aengus spat in the dust and stretched himself out on his belly so he could peer past the stones into the vale below. "Davin won't make it until dark," he said. "I need to get down to him."

"Look at the ground between the trees and the pond," Redmond said. "There's no cover. You'd never reach him."

"Then we rush the trees," Aengus said.

"If you want to stay alive," Redmond said with exaggerated calm, "you'll wait until dark." He settled himself behind the wall to study the copse of trees.

"There's only one," Aengus said.

"How do you know that?" Redmond asked. He couldn't help but

The Hidden Archer

wonder if Neahl was down there too, bleeding out from some terrible wound. It galled him to be trapped. What if there was only one archer? One of them might reach him. It was a risk, but . . .

"Well, if we sit here, they'll just encircle us," Aengus said.

"They might."

"Then we can't stay here."

Redmond lay on his back to peek around the other side of the stone pile for a better view. The copse of trees stood forty paces away. An easy shot for a good archer. There were patches of heather and grass between them, but nothing that would give them cover. He considered making a dash for the horses down by the pond and using them for protection. But the horses were more than thirty paces from the stone wall and unfamiliar with them or their scent. The horses would spook. It would be suicide. Unless something changed, the stone wall was the best chance they had of surviving.

"Water," someone called from the battlefield. The ravens cawed and fluttered their wings.

"I'm going," Aengus said.

Redmond grabbed him. "Wait," he said.

They knew nothing about the enemy that threatened them, but the fact that he was still there disturbed Redmond. Why had the archer remained behind? Why hadn't he fled with the rest of the raiding party? The Salassani didn't hang around battlefields. The birds always drew too much attention and gave them away.

The only possible answer was that it was a trap and there was more than one. The archer's job could be to pin them down while others crept up to finish them. It was the kind of thing the Salassani would do.

Redmond craned his head around to scan the ridgeline. His horse was trained to warn him if someone was around, but the horse was too far away for him to hear it.

Aengus jerked free of Redmond's grasp and rose to his feet. Two arrows whistled toward him. The shafts arced over the heather. Aengus spun to face them, but Redmond kicked his feet out from underneath him, sending him sprawling atop the pile of stones. The idiot didn't even have the sense to jump aside.

Aengus scrambled down behind the stones as another arrow slammed into his shoulder. He cursed and grabbed at the bloody shaft.

"You're an easy target," Redmond said.

Aengus let out a stream of curses, some of which Redmond had never heard. Writhing in pain and frustration, Aengus flopped down on his back behind the stone pile, snapped the arrow shaft, and cast it aside.

"I'll kill him," Aengus growled.

"Not from here you won't," Redmond said. He belly-crawled over to inspect Aengus's wound. The arrow had embedded itself in the bone.

"Hold still and I'll try to get it out," he said, though he knew the shaft would likely pull free from the point.

"Leave me alone," Aengus said. He jerked on the shaft until it came free. To Redmond's surprise the point came with it, followed by a gush of crimson blood. Aengus craned his neck to peer at the wound before clamping a hand over it. With time and the proper equipment Redmond could have done much to ensure that the wound healed without infection. But crouching behind a wall covered in dust, there was little he could do.

When he reached to tear a strip of cloth from Aengus's tunic to make a bandage, Aengus jerked away from him.

"Leave me alone," Aengus said again.

"It's your life," Redmond mumbled as he crawled away from Aengus's side. He rolled onto his back and stared up into the clear blue sky where the ravens floated in lazy circles. Aengus was a fool. That much he had proved. Two arrows had been shot at Aengus. Either there was more than one archer, or the archer had shot two arrows at one time. It was an old shooting trick that was fun to watch but of little battlefield use. Still, could he rely on that assessment?

"We can make it back to our horses," Aengus said.

"I think that archer, or archers, just proved that they aren't likely to miss again. They have your range now."

"We have to do something," Aengus growled. "Those men are dying down there."

"I'm aware of that," Redmond said. "So, we watch, and we wait. Come dark, things will shift in our favor."

"That's hours away."

Redmond didn't bother to respond. That much was obvious. Aen-

The Hidden Archer

gus cursed and complained and fidgeted as the sun slipped westward until it dipped behind the Aveen Mountains, casting long, mournful shadows over the scene.

The calls for water became weaker as the sun beat down upon them. Redmond had to resist the temptation to plug his ears to shut out the horrible moans and entreaties for help. The endless buzzing of the flies galled him. It was all he could do not to give in to Aengus's pleas and rush the copse of trees. His sweat soaked his clothes and trickled into the dirt. His mouth felt woolly, and his tongue stuck to the roof of his mouth. They would have to escape tonight.

Redmond busied himself with memorizing the landscape around them, searching for any movement or noise or object or smell that didn't belong. He studied the copse of trees so that he would know where each boulder lay, and he tried to imagine where he would hide if he were the archer in the trees.

A raven ruffled its wings where it perched on the top of one of the twisted junipers as another joined it. Redmond focused his attention on them. The birds could be resting as they waited their turn to feed, but their presence filled him with suspicion. Would they land so close to a living man? Any movement from a human should send them flapping and squawking. But they didn't stir. The birds gave no sign that anyone was hidden there in the trees.

Had the archers fled? Had they left to circle around behind them? If the men in the trees were going to attack, surely they would have done so by now. They had to know that darkness would even the odds considerably.

As the light of day faded, Aengus rose up on his good elbow and peered over the wall.

"I think they're gone," he said.

Redmond didn't reply. He had grown weary of Aengus's constant complaints and empty theories.

"I'm going down there," Aengus said.

"I would wait until dark," Redmond said.

He studied the ridge above them and tested the air with his nose for anything that would warn him. The stench of death still lingered in the valley. Nothing seemed amiss. Even the shy, little warblers sang loud and clear from among the heather.

Aengus stuck his head above the rock pile. Nothing happened. He progressively exposed larger parts of his body until he was kneeling in full view of the copse of junipers.

"No one's there," he said.

Aengus stood.

Redmond braced himself for the shriek of an arrow, but nothing happened. Aengus grinned at him and loped down to the pond.

He knelt beside Davin and said something to him. Then he crawled to the pond, cupped water in his hand and dribbled it into his brother's mouth. Redmond placed an arrow on the string of his bow and studied the copse of trees, ready to shoot if he got the chance. He searched the rocks and the ridgeline. Maybe he had been wrong. Maybe the Salassani had already gone. Maybe *he* had been the fool.

A movement flashed in the darkest shadows of the trees.

The ravens rose into the air with shrieks of surprise.

"Aengus!" Redmond yelled as he rose to one knee and sent an arrow into the copse of trees where he had seen the flash of movement.

He dropped back behind the pile of stones and stared helplessly as Aengus raised his head in time to catch the Salassani arrow in the chest.

Aengus grunted and fell sideways to writhe in the dirt for a moment before he jerked himself to his knees and yanked the arrow from his chest.

Redmond glanced up at the trees again. His broadhead had screeched as it ricocheted off a boulder. He nocked another arrow on his bow. He half-expected a mob of Salassani warriors to come screaming over the hill, but nothing happened.

Blood pumped from Aengus's wound. The fool should have left the arrow in.

Redmond hunkered behind the stones, racked with indecision. Every honorable bone in his body wanted to go to the men's aid. He had considerable skill as a healer, and he hated to see men die needlessly. But to go to them now was to share their fate. He knew this deep down in his bones. He might be able to rush the trees in the fading light and by some stroke of luck survive, but the odds were not in his favor.

Aengus thrashed in his death struggle. The parched earth drank his blood. Redmond couldn't save him from the wound in his chest,

The Hidden Archer

but he might be able to ease his pain by hastening his death.

Redmond raised his bow, canting it sideways so the limb wouldn't strike the ground or the stone wall. It was an easy shot. It would be the humane thing to do. Aengus would thank him for ending his suffering. One arrow through his throat, and he would bleed out fast. It would only take a few minutes for him to die.

At the last moment, Redmond changed his target, and the arrow buried itself deep behind a horse's front shoulder.

The horse reared and slipped in the mud.

It thrashed back to its feet and staggered out of the pond before it fell a few feet from where Aengus struggled.

Redmond launched himself from behind the stone wall, crouching low, running in a zig-zag pattern.

He dove behind the body of the still-quivering horse as an arrow slapped into the horse's belly.

The stink of bile and horse mingled with the smell of blood.

Redmond reached around the horse, grabbed Aengus's foot, and dragged him behind the horse.

Aengus opened his eyes.

His face had gone ashen white, his lips blue.

Blood dribbled from his mouth.

Redmond had to work from his belly as he tried to stop the bleeding.

He cut away Aengus's tunic and stuffed a wad of cloth into the wound, but it was too late.

Aengus grabbed his hand. His lips moved, but no sound came out. He squeezed Redmond's hand as a single tear trickled down his cheek into his ear.

His strength gave way, and his hand went limp.

Redmond tried to still the rising anger that burned his face. It had been foolhardy to risk his life for a dying man—especially one as asinine as Aengus. The Salassani had been waiting for this. He had deliberately withheld his shot until Aengus had exposed himself. Now he had drawn Redmond from the only real cover in the entire valley. Redmond was in more danger now than he had been all day. Aengus's brother still breathed not ten feet away—ten feet too far for Redmond to help him. Redmond ground his teeth in frustration and positioned himself so that he could peek over the horse's neck at the copse of trees.

The shadows stretched along the ground. It would be dark soon, though the darkness would only last until the moon rose to expose him to his enemies. If Redmond hoped to avoid spending the night amid the stench of the horse and of death, he needed to do something.

"Hey," he called in the Salassani language. "Why don't you come out, and we can finish this?"

A long silence ensued, and Redmond thought the man wouldn't answer, when a high-pitched voice called out, "I've got time."

Well, the Salassani had that right. Time was on his side. Redmond had not slept for over thirty-six hours. He'd had no food or water since they arrived at the vale. His mind was sluggish. Weakness had already crept into his limbs. The longer he waited, the worse he would get.

"How many are you?" he shouted.

"Enough," the man replied.

Redmond smiled. That meant there was only one, as he had suspected.

"Look," Redmond said, "I'm not interested in this war. All I want to do is ride out of here alive."

"You and me both," the Salassani said.

"That's easily arranged," Redmond said. "You simply ride away, and I will go my own way." He thought he heard a snort.

"If I thought I could trust an Alamani, I might consider it."

"So, ride away," Redmond said. "I won't follow."

A long pause ensued, and Redmond allowed his hopes to rise. Maybe the man would simply leave. Maybe all he had needed to do all along was talk to him. Why was it that the Salassani and the Alamani always believed the worst of each other? If they would stop killing and start talking, maybe these foolish wars could be avoided.

"I can't," the Salassani said.

Redmond barely heard it. What could that mean? Was the man under orders? Was he wounded? Had he lost his horse?

The gray of evening faded as Redmond puzzled over this brief conversation. Soon, he could no longer see the copse of trees. He had to make his move before the moon had risen or he would be trapped there all night.

The Hidden Archer

Redmond yanked off one of Aengus's boots, grasped his bow and his last two arrows in his left hand and prepared to bolt. He took a deep breath and tossed Aengus's boot out into the pool of water. As the splash sounded, he lunged to his feet and scrambled back up the rise. The whine of an arrow rushed toward him. It bit into the fleshy part of his arm above the elbow and behind the bone. He dove for the pile of stones as another arrow whistled overhead.

This archer was good. Even in the inky darkness before the moon had risen, he had been able to judge distance and speed. Redmond had been lucky this time. He grimaced in pain at the wound in his arm. It would become stiff and make it difficult to shoot, but it wasn't serious. He broke off the end of the arrow and pulled the broken shaft through. He didn't have any water to cleanse the wound, so he wrapped it with a strip of cloth as best he could and tried to ignore the ache as he prepared for his next move.

It was about thirty paces to the top of the ridge, almost as far as it was to the copse of trees. The Salassani would expect him to try to escape since his chances of survival seemed greater in that direction, so Redmond decided to approach the copse of trees.

By now, the landscape lay shrouded in darkness. Night owls hooted. Crickets chirped. Off in the distance, wolves called to each other. The cool air was refreshing after a day in the burning sun.

Had Neahl lived to see this night? Would Redmond live to see another? His mind drifted to Lara and her blonde hair and brown eyes. She would have called him a fool for what he was about to do. She would have been right. Only a fool would find himself pinned down by a single archer in the open heathland. She had begged him to stay out of this war, to let Neahl chase his own demons.

Scraping together a small pile of dirt, Redmond spat in it until he had enough mud to spread over his face and the back of his hands. It took a while because his mouth was so dry. He couldn't afford to have the white of his face revealed him to his enemy.

The Salassani would know that this was the most dangerous part of the night for him, and he would be alert and watching.

Redmond ripped a dried heather bush from the sandy soil and grasped it in his right hand. He held his bow and arrows in his left. Then he inched his way out from behind the only protection he had. It was risky, but what choice did he have? Redmond kept the heather bush in front of his face, hoping it would break up his profile as he crawled forward on his belly an inch at a time, expecting any minute to hear the screech of the flying shaft penetrate the stillness. He had never felt so exposed and vulnerable. From this position and at this range, he would not be able to avoid an arrow shot at him.

The copse of trees was no longer visible, but he had memorized the landscape. Minutes slipped by as he made his agonizing way across the vale. Sand and stickers crawled inside his shirt to chafe his skin. Unseen stones scraped his knuckles. The bitter taste of heather clung to his lips. He crept forward a foot or two and then waited before moving on.

When he had covered three fourths of the distance and the copse of trees had become a dark blob against the black sky, he heard quiet mumbling. He paused to listen, but a breeze rustled through the branches of the juniper. It soon passed and the normal noises of the sleeping heathland returned.

Redmond rolled to his back so that his left arm could stretch out toward the copse of trees. It would be only a few more minutes before the moon would rise over the eastern horizon and cast its glow over his head and onto the copse of trees. He would only have time for one arrow—one chance. If he missed, his life's blood would water the heathland.

He nocked an arrow and held it on the string with his forefinger as the fingers of his right hand searched for a rock. They closed around a fist-sized stone. The white light of the nearly-full moon splashed into the vale, bathing the world in a cool light. What had been black, hulking figures in the darkness took shape. The pile of boulders materialized from out of the night. Redmond held still as the light washed over him, fighting the gut-twisting fear that this would be the last moon he would ever see.

When the moon had fully illuminated the pile of boulders and trees in front of him, Redmond tossed his rock into them, grabbed the string of his bow, and drew it back as far as he could.

A head and shoulders snapped into view above a boulder.

Redmond released the string.

The head jerked back down, but it was too late.

Redmond heard the awful slap of an arrow penetrating flesh.

A grunt sounded.

The Hidden Archer

Redmond sprang to his feet and sprinted forward.

He dropped his bow and drew his sword as he scrambled over the boulders.

He leapt into a wide crevice amid the boulders where a gnarled old juniper reared its head.

Redmond's heart raced, and he tensed in preparation for battle.

What he found brought him up short.

Before him sprawled the body of a young man, maybe fifteen or sixteen, with an arrow through his neck. He lay draped over the body of an older man in his late thirties. The older man cradled the young man's head in his arms as the boy's blood drenched his clothes. Redmond raised his sword, then lowered it. A sick regret tightened his stomach.

The older man stared at Redmond with an expressionless face. He had a make-shift bandage on his head and a splint on his leg. His dark hair spilled from under the bandage. The muscles in his jaw twitched.

Redmond stepped back as he understood the implications of what he was seeing. He had been talking to a boy. The boy was the archer and couldn't leave because he had been protecting the older man. Redmond swallowed the knot that rose in his throat. He sheathed his sword.

"May I?" he asked, pointing to the boy. The man studied him and then nodded.

Redmond lifted the boy away and stretched him out on the dirt.

"What was his name?" he asked.

"Bodhi, my son," the man said. His voice was thick with emotion, but his face remained expressionless.

Redmond bowed his head. War was such a waste. How many had died fighting in battles that did not concern them?

"I'm sorry," he said. "I didn't know he was a boy."

"It is the way," the man said.

Redmond glanced up. That was the standard Salassani response to any setback. They simply accepted what they could not change. It was the way of life for things to change.

"Who are you?" Redmond asked.

"Mortegai," the man said. "From the high Daven Fens."

"You laid the ambush?"

"Yes. It is the way."

"Did you see a big, bearded man with a crippled hand?"

Mortegai nodded. "We know him. He likes to collect ears." He studied Redmond. "Are you his brother?"

Redmond stood. "Was he alive?"

"That one isn't so easy to kill," Mortegai said. "He was here. But I was injured and didn't see which way he went."

Redmond considered the man. His son probably owed his skill as an archer to him. Redmond respected men who disciplined themselves enough to excel at their craft.

"I'll help you bury him," he said.

Mortegai shook his head. "No. Go tend to your friends. He is beyond our aid."

Redmond studied him for a moment before he climbed out of the circle of boulders with a troubled heart. If he had been born in some rich man's mansion, maybe he wouldn't need to be a soldier. If he had been raised in a city with a shoemaker for a father, maybe his hands wouldn't be stained with the blood of this young man. But he had been born a poor farmer who had been forced into the role of a warrior by a Salassani raid on his village. Redmond retrieved his and Aengus's horses and led them down into the vale.

Two men were still alive, including Aengus's brother Davin, so he built up a fire, heated water to clean their wounds and to cook a meal. He gathered what horses he could find and picketed them near the puddle.

After treating the men's wounds and giving them water to drink, only Davin came around enough to be talk. Redmond spooned broth into the other's mouth hoping to get some nourishment into him, while Davin nibbled at a biscuit.

"What happened?" Redmond asked.

Davin paused with the biscuit an inch from his mouth. The light of the fire flickered in his eyes.

"Jaxon was the lead scout trailing the Salassani," he said. "He came back and told us the trail was clear for another mile, so we just rode into the vale to water the horses."

"You think Jaxon betrayed you?" Redmond asked.

Jaxon was a Salassani who had been exiled from his people and had joined the Alamani as a scout and spy. He had always been an

The Hidden Archer

irascible fellow, but Redmond didn't think him capable of betraying them to the Salassani. After all, the Salassani had put out one of his eyes in punishment of the crime for which he had been banished.

Davin paused to swallow. Then he pointed to one of the bodies that sprawled facedown beside the pond with two arrows in his back. Redmond hadn't noticed when he checked the bodies, but now he realized it was Jaxon's son.

"If he did betray us," Davin said, "I don't think things went according to plan."

Redmond considered the young man's body. He was barely eighteen, and he was probably one of the first to die. Jaxon must have been pressed hard in the battle to abandon his own son.

Davin's gaze strayed to where his brother Aengus lay in the shadow of the horse where Redmond had left him.

"I'm sorry," Redmond said. "I tried to save him."

Davin shook his head as if he didn't want to discuss it. He raised his gaze to stare at the copse of trees still bathed in the light of the moon.

"They came screaming out of the heather," he said, "like a band of demons. Neahl and Tyg cut a gap through them and held it while the others escaped."

Redmond glanced around at the dark shapes of twenty men that lay dead amid the trampled grass. There were a few Salassani, but most were his own men. At least Neahl had escaped.

"You rest," Redmond said. "When your stomach holds the biscuits, I'll give you some stew."

Davin nodded as he nibbled at the biscuit.

Redmond rose and carried a bowl of warm stew to Mortegai. He found him still leaning against the rock with a hand on his son's head.

"I trained him," Mortegai said with a nod to the boy. "Since he was a child, he always wanted to be a warrior."

"I'm sorry," Redmond said, as he handed him the bowl. It seemed nothing Redmond had done in the last two days had gone well.

"Why do we do this?" Mortegai asked. "Why do we fight and kill and die for some other man's dream? What will any of us gain when the kings have ended their squabbles?" He pointed at Redmond with the spoon. "You and me? What do we get out of it but broken hearts and ruined lives?"

41

Redmond had no answer for him. He had long thought the kings and nobles should do their own fighting and leave the people out of it.

"There are a couple of extra horses," Redmond said. "I'll bring them to you as soon as it gets light, and you can take him home."

"I won't make it," Mortegai said. "I can't mount a horse like this."

Redmond nodded. The man was right.

"I'll be back for the bowl," he said, rising to his feet.

The next morning dawned in a display of corals and pinks that distracted Redmond's attention from making the travois. He paused with the leather strap in his hands as a streak of lavender cut through the clouds. A blue haze draped itself over the rolling hills and crept down towards the shadows of the Laro Forest. Redmond glanced at the corpses of men and horses that littered the valley and pondered on the contrast. It seemed so wrong that such a beautiful morning should rise over the stinking corpses of men who would never hold their children or kiss their wives again.

Redmond jerked the cord tight and finished with a clove hitch. Had he known it was one boy and an injured man hiding up there in the rocks, he would have made different choices. But he had learned long ago that you couldn't second-guess yourself in war. He had done the only thing he could under the circumstances. Redmond hitched the makeshift travois to one of the horses and dragged it up to where Mortegai still leaned with his back to the boulder. Redmond lifted the boy onto the back of another horse and tied him in place before helping Mortegai onto the travois.

He collected the boy's weapons and placed them next to Mortegai before he gave him a couple of waterskins and what food he could spare. Then he tied the horses together so they wouldn't become separated. Salassani ponies knew how to find their way home.

Mortegai's gaze followed Redmond as he worked. "You're a strange Alamani."

Redmond scratched the back of his head. "I don't fight because I hate," he said. "I fight because I must."

"What shall I call you?" Mortegai asked.

"I'm Redmond," he said. "A simple archer."

Raising his hand in a salute, Mortegai said, "May your quiver ever be full, and may the lords of the Keldi protect you from harm."

The Hidden Archer

Redmond slapped the lead horse's flank, and it set out, kicking up little clouds of dust. The boy's body draped over the back of the lead horse while the second horse dragged the wounded Salassani north into the heathland.

Mortegai kept his gaze on Redmond until the horses dropped over the rise and disappeared. Redmond had let his enemy go. Would their paths ever cross again, and, if so, who would ride away and who would be left to molder amid the heather?

AUTHOR'S NOTE

The inspiration for *The Hidden Archer* came from my viewing of the 2017 movie, entitled *The Wall*. I wondered what an archer like Redmond would do if pinned down by another archer in an exposed position. Obviously, the different technology would create new opportunities and limitations. The story allowed me to explore Redmond's character more as I prepared to make his relationship with Lara one of the key parts of Book II *Betrayal*. Redmond and his exploits in the southland are the focus of Book V *Windemere*. This story helps explain his attitude toward nobility and warfare that he imparts to Brion in Books I and II.

This is also the ambush that turned Jaxon against Neahl. Though Jaxon was to blame for missing the ambush as he scouted, he never forgave Neahl for his son's death. Davin didn't know it, but Neahl had saved Jaxon's life during the ambush, which only made Jaxon more bitter. Jaxon finally takes his revenge on Neahl in Book II *Betrayal*.

WAR OF THE
ONE-EYED WOMAN

Cut her down, Edrick."

My father's voice was hard. His hand slipped to the hilt of his sword, and the muscles in his jaw worked. He was a big man with broad shoulders and long, graying hair. People said if the Carpentini were ever to have a king, it would be my father.

I rushed to the old, swayback nag and stared up at the once-beautiful face of my sister, Aila. Her skin had always been fair, but now it was pasty-white, like the chalk pits down by the sea. Her long, curly hair was a tangled mess, and her clothes were stained and torn.

But the worst thing—the thing that made the bitterness rise in my throat—was the dark, oozing hole where her left eye should have been. The other eye, still bright green, glistened in the waning light of the summer evening. Aila stared at me with the one eye as if she expected me to say something. It was the expression she used when she hadn't liked one of my jokes.

She had been mounted backwards on the old mare and tied into place with her arms encircling a small, wriggling bundle. The strong reek of urine and filth overpowered the smell of horse sweat. A knot formed in my stomach, and heat rushed into my face. How many days had they made her ride like this?

I jerked my knife from its sheath and sliced through the straps that bound her to the saddle. She sagged and slid toward me. Two men rushed forward to help me pull her from the horse and lay her on the ground in the lane before my father's two-story cottage. Her clothes were covered in human filth and dark blood.

Our neighbor woman ran up and pressed a waterskin to Aila's lips as I worked on the straps that bound the bundle to her. Aila gulped at the water, but when I tried to lift the bundle away, she snatched at it and hugged it close. The bundle made a sound, and a tiny fist punched through the wrappings.

I sat back on my haunches and stared in confusion. It didn't make any sense. Why would Donach send her back if she had given him an heir?

A year ago, my father had made an alliance with the great Bracari chieftain, Donach, to put an end to the long feud between us. According to the ancient law, my sister would live with him as man and wife though they had not wed. If she bore him an heir before a year and a day had passed, he would marry her, and the alliance would be final. If she did not, he would return her to us, and the bargain would be void.

The way my sister clutched the child she had borne to Donach revealed the ferocious love she had for it. Why would he mutilate her and send her back in such shame and disgrace?

I glanced up as the Bracari man, who had so casually walked into our village leading the old, swaybacked mare, approached my father. He touched his fingers to his forehead in the Carpentini greeting and bowed. My father did not return the gesture.

"My master bids me deliver you this message," the man said. His voice carried the lilting speech of the Bracari, and his clothes were the loose, dun-colored linen favored by them. He glanced around apprehensively at the gathering of sullen, grim faces. When my father still said nothing, the man continued.

"My master thanks you for the service of your one-eyed nag. As she could only bear him a useless cow, he has no more need of her services."

My father jerked his sword from its sheath and snapped it at the man's neck. The man flinched as the sword stopped with the blade resting on his throat. A trickle of red blood dribbled onto the blade. The man's eyes were wide, but he didn't cower.

"You tell your master," my father said, "that I will feed his carcass to the ravens and the wolves before the moon is new." Then he kicked the man in the stomach and sent him sprawling in the dirt.

The man scrambled to his feet and scurried up the road, but my father called after him. "Take the nag with you."

The man glanced at Aila as if he wasn't sure which nag my father meant. For one sinking moment, I wasn't sure myself. But the man decided he must have meant the horse and snatched the reins to yank the horse after him.

My father waited until the man was out of earshot before he faced the crowd. "The Carpentini go to war," he said.

Then he glanced down at Aila. A tear had left a stain on her cheek. "Carry her inside," he said.

This time his voice was soft. He stared at her as if he couldn't look away, as if this was his worst nightmare come true.

I lifted her into my arms, fighting the horrible, sickening feeling in my chest. In her starved condition, Aila couldn't weigh more than ninety-pounds. She was barely nineteen and already her life was ruined.

If I had been born four years earlier, I would have been the one sacrificed for the peace. I would have taken a Bracari wife. But I was still only sixteen and too young to be allowed to sire children.

Instead, my quiet, sensitive sister had been sent away to live with my father's worst enemy—a man known for his violent temper and pleasure in other people's suffering. I had argued against the match, but she was the last daughter of childbearing age my father had. The other two had married and lived in different villages. I was the youngest and the only male.

I carried Aila upstairs to the room my mother had insisted on leaving vacant for her, wondering why Mother hadn't come out to the street when Aila had been led in. But Mother was already in the room, turning down the bedsheets. A basin of steaming water stood on the side table by a pile of clean cloth. Mother never said much, so I wasn't surprised by the silence with which she greeted her youngest daughter. She waited until I had settled Aila onto the bed and then shooed me from the room.

By the time I reached the street again, a party of sixty or seventy men had already gathered. People scampered about and horsemen galloped in and rode out in a flurry of activity. My father had his bow strung and his quiver strapped to his back. His traveling satchel hung over his shoulder, opposite his sword. I shouldered my way through the milling crowd until I stood beside him.

"We go now," he was saying. "Donach will be expecting a large war party that would take us days to organize. We will strike now to draw him out."

"What if he's already waiting for us?" Gerald asked.

My father smiled. "He won't be expecting us to attack from the north."

"Go around behind them?" someone asked.

"I'm coming," I said.

My father glanced at me and shook his head.

"No, Edrick. I need you here."

He grabbed my arm and pulled me away from the crowd.

"I want you to take Aila and her—" he paused, "her baby, and your mother to Aveen. If I know anything about Donach, he's already on the move. I've ordered the village to be fortified, and an army will be gathering in the foothills, while I swing east and north. If we're lucky, we'll catch him between us." He pulled me to a stop. "If something goes wrong, I want you to live," he said. "You will take my place."

People had said I looked like my father, with the same dark hair and eyes and the large build, but I was too young to take his place. Surely, he could see that. I was afraid that he was going to sacrifice himself to kill Donach.

I protested, but he squeezed my arm in a vice-like grip.

"I tried to end this feud peacefully," he growled, "by giving that scoundrel my own daughter. Now I will end it in blood or die trying."

A rider pounded up the road and leapt from his saddle. My father turned to speak with him, and I was forgotten. I gazed out at the rising, green hills of the moor, spotted with purple heather and jagged, rock outcrops. The Aveen Mountains rose up purple and blue on the eastern horizon. Donach would either come through the foothills to cloak his movements, or he would rush straight south over the moor to catch us unawares.

My father was sending me to the city of Aveen—really a large village nestled in one of the few navigable bays along the rocky, western coast. But how could I go? What would the men think of me running away from a battle? I was big enough and old enough to fight. Everyone would call me a coward behind my back.

I faced the cottage. Figures moved around in the upper room. I ground my teeth. Regardless of what Father said, I was going to do my part. No Bracari could abuse my sister like that and go unpunished.

A servant brought my father his horse. He sprang into the saddle. Catching my eye, he nodded to me once and rode off with the band of men that had gathered.

I raced to the cottage and leapt up the stairs two at a time. A servant had come out of Aila's room, and I caught the door before it closed.

"May I come in?" I asked.

"Come," Mother said.

I found Aila sitting in bed propped up against the wall. A cloth bandage had been wrapped around her head to cover the missing eye. Momma had washed the filth away and dressed her in clean clothing. The color had returned to her cheeks. She tried to smile.

I sat beside her and grasped her hand. "Why?" I asked. "You gave him a child."

Her lip quivered. "He's a brute," she said. "He would only accept a son."

Mother clicked her tongue, and I glanced at her. She was cradling the child in her arms and rocking back and forth.

"What's her name?" I asked.

"I haven't given her one," Aila said. "I wasn't sure either of us would live."

"Gwyneth," my mother said. "We will call her Gwyneth."

Aila smiled. "I like that."

"Papa wants me to take you both out of the village," I said. I didn't say anything about Aveen because I had other plans, and I didn't want Momma to know. Not yet.

Mother's head snapped up. She stared at me for a moment, then placed Gwyneth in Aila's arms, and strode from the room.

"Where?" Aila asked.

"Aveen," I said.

"Why?" Aila's face was tense. I still struggled to get used to how lopsided she looked with that big bandage where her beautiful eye should have been.

"He thinks Donach is coming for us."

Aila nodded. "Donach wants the entire Aveen Moor to range his cattle on," she said. "He used me as an excuse to push the rest of the Carpentini south. He knows the Alamani are pushing us north, and he says now is the time to seize what he can."

I clenched my jaw tight and glanced down at the baby. She couldn't be more than a few weeks old. I reached out to stroke her soft head. She had Aila's delicate features, but the thin tuft of hair was black, like Donach's, and she had his strong chin.

"You're not going to take us to Aveen, are you?" Aila whispered.

I shook my head without looking at her.

"You can't go after Donach, Edrick," she said. "He's a dangerous man. Let Papa handle it."

"Papa's not thinking straight," I said. "If I were Donach, I would have been right behind my messenger. I think he's out there watching us right now."

Aila's face paled. "He'll kill me," she said. "He said he would once I was no more use to him."

My throat constricted, and I lunged to my feet. "I'm taking you to the flume," I said. "There's a little hunting lodge there. You'll be safe until this is over."

"Don't," Aila said. A tear trickled from her eye. "He'll kill you. You don't stand a chance."

"I'm a man now," I said.

Aila wiped at the tear that trickled down her cheek. "You don't know him."

Mother came in with one of the women from the village. I gave Aila a stern look, warning her not to tell Mother that I was disobeying Father. She frowned, but held her tongue. Momma shooed me away again, so I left her to get Aila ready to travel. Donach wasn't the only one who could be crafty. If I was right and he came for us tonight, I would be prepared for him.

We set out under the cover of darkness. I carried my short horn bow and a full quiver of arrows. My sword dangled from my hip, and my boot knife bulged against my calf muscle. Another knife was strapped to my forearm. Mother carried Gwyneth, and Aila rode beside me. She was still weak, but I wasn't taking them far.

We entered the bottom of the flume where the boulders piled up on top of each other—hulking shadows in the moonless night. The walls of the flume rose up on either side of us. Great clumps of shaggy moss clung to the dark stone dripping with little rivulets of water which fed the stream that bounced among the boulders. The

War of the One-Eyed Woman

horses slowed to pick their way as the shadows deepened, and the world closed in around us.

The air smelled alive with that deep, earthy aroma only a forest has. Oaks and beeches rose above us and rattled their leaves in the evening breeze.

I had always loved the flume. It was a place of refuge and mystery to me. Now it would protect my sister and her baby from the monster who had tortured them. I left them in the hunting lodge with plenty of firewood and supplies to last a couple of weeks. Mother had carried along a lance tied to her saddle, and, before I left, she pulled a short sword from her blankets. I nodded to her. My mother was a real Carpentini woman, like the women in the old tales. She was strong and brave, willing to do whatever it took to protect her family.

"Be careful," Aila said.

Momma gave me a calculated look, pulled me into a hug and said, "Be a man, son. But don't be a fool."

I swallowed the lump that rose in my throat. She knew what I was planning to do.

I slipped back into the blackness of the flume that had come alive with frogs and crickets calling to one another. The creek gurgled as my horse carefully selected her path amid the stones with her head hung low to the trail.

A fox called. A flutter of wings rushed overhead. I was sure that Donach would come tonight. He was bold and daring. It was the sort of thing he would do. Thinking of him made the night seem more hostile, more alert and intent on my every move, as if someone were watching me. I shook off the feeling and kept moving. I knew where Donach would come through. I just needed to catch him before he passed.

When I reached the pile of rubble at the mouth of the flume, I dismounted, tied strips of sheep's wool to my horse's hooves, and led her into the night. I knew this land better than I knew the lines on my own hands. If Donach was coming tonight, he would come through the glen and on into the depression by the river. I would be waiting for him.

Before I reached the glen, I tied my horse, strung my bow, and placed three arrows in my left hand—careful to avoid cutting myself with the sharp broadheads. I crawled to the edge of the glen. The stars twinkled in the black sky, but nothing stirred. In fact, no sound lifted on the night air.

My blood raced. Someone was out there or had been there recently. The forest knew this, and it held its breath in anticipation. I worked my way around to the path where I discovered the clear signs of a troop of men passing. I had found them.

I returned to my horse, mounted, and worked my way down to the cutaway by the river where I dismounted again. I crawled on my belly to the edge and peered over. The hulking shapes of men shifted about in the darkness. I nocked an arrow. If I could find him and stick an arrow in his heart right now, I could end this before anyone else got hurt. My pulse pounded in my ears, and I trembled in anticipation.

Leaves rustled behind me. Terror gripped my throat as I rolled. The shape of a man loomed above me, black against the stars. I plucked the bowstring, rolled again, and came to my feet.

My arrow thumped into a body. A man grunted in pain, but I knew my weak shot wouldn't be lethal. I nocked another arrow, searching for a way back to my horse.

Something hard slammed into the side of my head. Pain exploded behind my eyes, and I staggered against a tree. I blinked as a shadow lunged for me.

I jerked the string without getting it to full draw, but the arrow bit into my enemy. The man growled in anger, and I ducked as the club swung for my head again.

I sprinted into the trees, but someone tackled me from the side, and we sprawled to the ground. I struggled to reach the knife strapped to my forearm. A heavy man pinned me to the ground while another stepped on my arm.

"Stop, ya dern fool."

I would have known that voice anywhere.

"Papa?" I said.

He bent close. "Where are they?" he demanded.

I tried to swallow the sickness that rose in my throat. My father hadn't figured wrong at all. He had been leaving a false trail by talking out loud about his plans back in the village.

He grabbed my shoulders and shook me. "Where are they?" he

demanded.

"In the flume," I said. "I thought it would be safer."

My father swore. "I told you to take them to Aveen for a reason," he snapped. "Get up."

I climbed to my feet, glad the darkness hid the shame on my face.

"Is anyone bad hurt?" my father asked.

I knew he wasn't referring to the knot on my head or the warm blood trickling down my neck.

"Edrick missed the vitals," someone said.

"Who did he hit?"

"Arnold and Bredlin."

"I'm sorry," I said.

"Sorry is no good to me," my father said. "You go back to the flume and get them out of there. Take them to Aveen."

"Why?" I asked.

"If you can follow a trail in the dark," my father said, "so can the Bracari."

My heart sank. I *had* left a trail all the way up the flume and back again. They would know that only one horse returned. How could I have been such a fool?

"Lotrel," a voice called. "The scouts are back."

My father jogged away into the night. I followed, desperate for news before I blundered off again. We dropped down into the cut-away.

"Speak," Papa said.

"Donach is before the village. He has 100 men with him."

"Where are the clans?" my father asked.

"We found no sign of them."

My father cursed again. "He's slipped us," he said. "Well, we'll pin him between us and the village then. Up men."

My father glanced at me. "Why are you still here?"

I spun and raced up the river, splashed through the shallows, scrambled up the cutaway, and worked my way back to my horse. I didn't try to conceal my movements. Not now. I had failed my father and placed my sister, her baby, and my mother in danger. I had to set things right. We could escape out the top of the flume and swing wide to circle west for Aveen.

When I entered the flume, no creature stirred. Everything but the bubbling brook had fallen silent. Dread encircled my heart. What had I done? I dismounted before I reached the hunting lodge and crept amid the jumble of boulders until I could make out its A-shaped shadow against the stone wall of the flume. The door stood ajar. The horses were gone.

A great emptiness filled my chest. I forgot everything else in my desperation to find out where they had gone. As I lunged forward across the open space between the creek and the hunting lodge, my foot snagged, and I crashed face-first on top of a body. Terror gripped my throat as I rolled free. My hand splashed in a puddle of warm liquid, and the odor of blood and sweat filled my nostrils.

"Please, no," I begged. "Please, no."

I knelt beside the body and bent close in the darkness, feeling the bulky shadow on the ground with trembling hands.

But it was wrong. The clothes were coarse. There was stubble on the face. It was a Bracari, and his blood hadn't grown cold.

I lunged to my feet and raced to the hunting lodge. The coals from the fire glowed red in the fireplace. The sparse furniture had been scattered. Mother's spear lay broken on the floor.

The supplies we had carried to the shack were smashed in the corner. The dark stains of something wet glistened red in the dim light of the coals.

I grabbed a stick from the kindling by the fireplace, ripped a blanket into strips, and wrapped them around the stick. I made a quick bird's nest of the pile of tinder, poked a coal from the fire into the nest, and blew until the bundle erupted into flames. Then I lit the strips of blanket. The ruined hut materialized into the dancing light of the torch.

I burst through the door and bent close to the ground, holding the rapidly-burning torch low, as I tried to figure out which way they had gone. Not ten paces from the shack, a torn and bloody fragment of the shawl in which Gwyneth had been wrapped lay pressed into the mud. Farther on, a trail of overturned moss and horse tracks showed they were heading up the flume.

Racing back to my horse, I jumped into the saddle. There was only one way out of the flume in that direction. They couldn't be too far ahead of me. The horse struggled to find her way amid the boulders, but the slowness of the pace galled me. It tore at my nerves, and I finally leapt from her back and pulled her along as I struggled up the flume. I would have left the horse behind if I hadn't known that after the flume ended there would be open ground to cover, and I would need all the speed I could muster.

After an hour of staggering and tripping my way over the rocky floor of the flume, I neared the outlet. The stars burned in the crack where the trees parted by the wide opening. The chill of the early morning air against my sweat-soaked clothes made me shiver. I slowed. Now was not the time to be a fool. I left my horse to pick her way after me, and I bent to hide in the shadows—to listen and to watch. When I could wait no longer, I crept through the gap.

The trees thinned, and the air lost the earthy mustiness of the flume. But it was still too dark to follow a trail closely. Once I was sure no one waited to ambush me, I retrieved my horse and worked my way up to the crest of the hill where the heathland spread out before me. The pale light of the coming dawn lightened the sky. Shadows took shape. Which way would they go? Would they head north for Bracari lands or west toward the sea? Or would they take them back to Donach so he could murder them all himself?

I glanced around, struggling to keep my impatience in check. I couldn't afford to lose their trail now because I didn't have the discipline to wait until I could see more clearly. My gaze focused on a hulking shape that lay against the trunk of a shriveled oak, when I realized it was a body. I bent close. It was another Bracari. He had a terrible wound on his neck. It looked as if he had been cut from behind, like an assassin might kill a man.

What puzzle was this? My mother was strong enough to do it, but if they were captured, how had she managed it? Did this mean they hadn't been captured but were fleeing and fighting still? My heart beat faster at the thought, and I hoped as I hadn't dared to hope all while I struggled up the flume.

I dropped to my hands and knees and crawled along until I found the trail. It ran through the trees and dropped over the lip of the hillside towards the broad valley spotted with clumps of juniper and pine. My heart sank. I would never catch them at this rate. I had lost more than half an hour puzzling out their trail. They were moving to the open heathland where their tracks would be hard to find and they could gallop their horses.

I sat back on my haunches. If my mother was fleeing, where would she go? She would go where my father had said they should go—to Aveen. I faced the western horizon. If I was wrong, they would die. But if I had to read their trail step-by-step, I would never catch them. Aila couldn't last long in her weakened condition. It was a miracle she was still going at all. I made my decision. I would ride to cut them off. Everything now depended on whether Aila had told my mother where father had wanted them to go.

A few minutes later, I was galloping hard through the heather. I hoped to catch them at the bridge south of the village. That was the nearest road to Aveen. The morning glow brightened to full light as the heathland passed beneath me. My eyes ached with lack of sleep and every muscle begged me to rest. But I kicked my horse on, though she was already starting to slow.

I found the bridge deserted when I reached it an hour later. The fresh horse tracks and the still-damp splashes of blood told me that I had guessed right and that someone was wounded. I kicked my horse into a wild dash and hadn't gone two hundred paces before they came into view.

Not thirty paces from me, Mother stood with her back to a boulder—the baby in one arm and her sword in the other hand. Aila lay crumpled on the road beside her horse, which stood with its head down, its sides heaving. Three Bracari were dismounting. Two advanced on my mother. A third stepped toward Aila's still form when a small figure dashed out of the underbrush that lined the creek and fell upon Aila with a shriek.

I whipped an arrow from my quiver, dropped my reins, and guided my horse with my knees. I bent my bow and shot one of the Bracari in the back before they could even spin to face me.

My second arrow found the other Bracari, but in my haste, I shot low. The arrow plunged into his belly.

The third Bracari spun and loosed an arrow at me, which I didn't have time to avoid. It buried itself in my horse's face with a sickening crack. My horse stumbled and fell.

I kicked free of the stirrups the way my father had trained me and landed on my feet.

My knees buckled. The arrows in my quiver snapped as I rolled, so I dropped my bow and swept my sword from its sheath.

War of the One-Eyed Woman

I came to me feet and sprinted toward the Bracari, desperate to cross the last ten paces before he could get off another shot. But he was already aiming at me. I was too close to avoid the arrow.

The small figure who had thrown himself on Aila rose up and raced toward the Bracari. It was a woman. I didn't pause to consider who it was.

All I could see was the Bracari devil standing over my sister with his arrow nocked ready to kill me before I could save her. The woman collided with the Bracari, and his arrow flew wide as he tumbled to the earth.

He kicked her off him and scrambled to his feet. But I was already there. He deflected my first blow. The clash of our swords rang amid the boulders. The back sweep of my blade bit so deep into his side that it jerked the sword from my grasp.

The Bracari staggered and lunged toward me in one last, desperate attempt to skewer me. I sidestepped his stroke and kicked his knees. He fell with a groan.

I rushed to Aila's side and lifted her into my arms. Tears slipped from my eyes as I carried her to the rock where mother had dropped the sword and set the baby down in the grass.

"I'm sorry," I stammered.

Aila opened her eye. The bandage had slipped off her head, and the black hole, where the other eye should have been, stared at me. A clear liquid dribbled from the corner of it.

"Isobel?" Aila asked, looking around.

I laid Aila on the ground and knelt beside her before glancing at my mother in confusion.

Momma shrugged. "I don't know who she is," she said. "But I'm not going to complain."

She walked to the horses. When Momma came back with her bag, a young woman was standing behind her. Momma bent to tend to Aila, so I rose to face the woman. She was a young Bracari who stared at me with wide eyes. Her dun-colored tunic was stained with blood and grime. Her hair was black and filled with bits of twigs and moss. She had a long, red gash on her cheek, and blood dribbled from the side of her mouth.

"Isobel," Aila said again, and I realized she was speaking to the Bracari woman. The woman knelt beside her and lifted her hand.

"Why?" Aila asked.

Isobel brushed a hair from Aila's face with a gentleness that surprised me.

"I couldn't stand what he did to you," Isobel said. "It was wrong. We all knew it was wrong."

"Thank you," Aila said and raised Isobel's hand to her lips.

"But how did you find us?" I said in confusion. "Donach doesn't take women on his raids."

Isobel scowled at me. "A woman can go anywhere a man can go."

"You followed him?"

"I followed Aila," Isobel said.

"It was you that killed the two Bracari I found back there?"

Isobel bowed her head. "Three," she said.

"I missed one?"

"Men always underestimate women," she said.

The baby fussed, and Isobel retrieved her from the ground where Momma had left her. She held her tight and sang softly to her.

While Momma cared for Aila, I checked the Bracari. The one with the arrow in his belly was still alive.

I kicked him onto his back.

"Finish me," he stammered.

"What are Donach's plans?" I demanded.

The Bracari clutched at the arrow shaft and yanked it out. Blood and bile gushed from the wound.

"It doesn't matter," he said. "Donach already attacked your village and another party hit Aveen this morning."

"Aveen?" I said in disbelief.

Now where was I to take the women? I needed to get them to safety so that I could go back to fight beside my father before it was too late. He needed to know that the men from Aveen wouldn't be coming to help.

"You Carpentini are finished," the Bracari said.

He stared up at me. "Now, kill me. I don't know anymore."

All the fight had left me. To kill in the heat of battle was one thing, but to kill a wounded, helpless man was quite another.

"I can't," I said.

The Bracari sneered. "This is why you lose your land," he said. "You are not man enough to do what needs to be done." He drew a knife from his sheath, and I turned away. I didn't want to see him do it.

I couldn't take the women to Aveen, and I couldn't take them back to our village. After Momma had treated Aila and Aila had suckled the baby, we remounted on the four least-winded horses, and I led them to the nearest village. It was small, but I hoped someone would be there. A few women and children met us with grim faces and frightened eyes. Despite their fear, they took the women in. I left them and raced across the moor back to my village. Back to my father.

It was high noon by the time I arrived to find the village burning. A few dogs trotted about, but no one was there, save several crumpled bodies scattered amid the smoking rubble. Great orange tongues of flame licked at the thatched roofs. My father's cottage was a smoldering ruin. Soot coated my tongue and throat. I was too late again. My whole world had evaporated in the course of one night.

I rode out toward the river where I had last seen my father. Maybe I could find someone who knew where he had gone. The shouts of battle and the crash of steel reached me before I could see the struggling men. I had retrieved my bow and the half dozen arrows that hadn't broken in the fall from my horse. I pulled an arrow from the quiver and nocked it. I dismounted and crept to the top of the rise. My heart skipped a beat, and my breath caught in my throat.

Hundreds of men locked in a bitter struggle over a narrow creek which flowed toward the river. Bodies lay scattered on the hillside. Wounded men groveled and cried out in agony. The Bracari had their backs to me, and the line of struggling men surged back and forth across the creek that flowed red with their blood. My father stood with his legs wide, wielding his sword with the incredible strength for which he was renowned. But he was alone, encircled by a growing crowd of Bracari. Donach was cutting his way through our men toward him.

At the sight of Donach's long, black hair billowing out behind him and his broad shoulders, something inside me snapped. Here was the man that had ruined my family and destroyed my village. Here was the man who had gouged out my sister's eye after a year of abusing her.

I mounted and kicked my Bracari horse into a gallop as I loosed my arrow into the back of a Bracari warrior. Then I slipped my bow over my head and drew my sword. I plunged into the midst of the battle, slashing and shoving my way toward my father.

Donach had closed with my father, and the men had backed off to give them room to duel. I tried to kick my horse toward them, but someone dragged me from my saddle.

My sword bounced from my hand as I hit the ground hard. I rolled and snatched my boot knife from its sheath as a Bracari bore down upon me.

Blood had sprayed his face, and, for one moment, I wondered whose blood it was. I dodged the sword stroke and rushed to close the distance. My knife scraped against his ribs as I buried it to the hilt. He fell to his knees, dragging my knife from my hand.

I shrugged my bow over my head and checked to make sure it wasn't broken. The horn was tough, and it had held. I whirled to find Donach as I snatched an arrow from my quiver.

It was broken. I tossed it aside and grabbed another. I nocked it and darted up the hill. All along the creek, the fighting slowed and came to a halt as the two parties separated to watch their leaders locked in mortal combat. I rushed past the last men, who stood panting with their swords dangling in their hands as if they were in a trance.

My father's sword slipped inside Donach's guard, but the injury was small. Donach screamed in fury and brought his sword down with such strength that he tore my father's sword from his hand.

I stopped, drew, and loosed. My arrow dove under Donach's up-raised arm and plunged into his armpit. The rush of jubilation that filled my chest at the sight of my arrow burying itself in Donach's side was quickly smothered.

A howl rose up around us, and the fighting recommenced. Bracari rushed to Donach's aid, and my father was swept along with them. The last I saw of him, he had his dagger in one hand, and his sword in the other.

My arrows ran out, so I grabbed up a fallen sword and launched myself into the cluster of men that surrounded my father. He had disappeared into the chaos.

The terror that he had already fallen gave desperate strength to my efforts. More Carpentini joined me, and, together, we fought the

War of the One-Eyed Woman

Bracari back across the creek. But I still couldn't find my father.

The final surge across the bloody creek and the loss of their leader sent the Bracari fleeing up the opposite hill. I let the other men pursue them. My father was there somewhere. I staggered up the hill, searching every face, terrified I would find his mangled body. Father's head and shoulders appeared above the heather as he dragged himself downhill to where Donach lay on his side.

I tried to run to him, but the weariness and trembling in my legs meant I could only stagger. Father reached Donach before I did. He shoved Donach over onto his back. Donach's chest still rose and fell. Only the fletchings of my arrow could be seen under his arm. With a wound like that, he wouldn't last long.

Donach opened his eyes and lifted a feeble hand. Father propped himself up on one elbow, raised his dagger and plunged it into Donach's eye. A gurgling cry of vengeance and anguish erupted from my father. Donach's body jerked and trembled before it lay still. My father's head drooped, and he sagged to the ground.

I reached him and lifted his head into my lap. He had so many wounds and was so covered in blood that I couldn't tell which one was the worst. I pressed my hands against a huge gash on his leg.

"Did you find them?" he asked.

I nodded, unable to speak. My whole body trembled. Weariness filled my heart.

"Are they safe?"

"Yes," I said. "The Bracari attacked Aveen. I took Mother, Aila, and Gwyneth to Reed's village."

"Gwyneth?" my father questioned.

"Mother named the baby Gwyneth," I said.

"I hope she brings Aila happiness," he said, "because I've brought Aila nothing but sorrow."

My father tried to swallow. His breathing became labored.

"Tell her I'm sorry," he said. "Tell her I wish I had never done it."

"She knows," I said.

"Edrick," my father said.

He placed a filthy, blood-stained hand on mine and lay still.

I bent over him as the bitter tears slipped down my cheeks. In the space of one night and one day, my whole world had been swamped in a river of blood. When I finally stood and gazed out over the bloody creek and the dead and dying men that littered the green hillside, I realized the Carpentini had been broken. We may have won the field, but we had lost so many men.

How would we recover? We had never been as numerous as the other tribes. Now we had ruined fields, destroyed villages, and hundreds of dead men. My mind turned to Gwyneth—the child of the man I had helped to kill. The child that had caused this war simply because she had been born a girl. Would anyone ever let her forget? Would anyone let her be Carpentini?

The slanting light of day cast a ray onto the creek where it gurgled red as it slipped among the bodies stretched amid the heather. The creek might eventually wash away the blood of this day. But it could never cleanse the damage done in this war caused by a one-eyed woman and her baby.

AUTHOR'S NOTE

While rummaging around doing research on my Scottish heritage, I came across the story of the "Wars of the One-Eyed Woman," which were a series of conflicts fought in 1601 on the Isle of Sky between the Clan MacDonald of Dunvegan and Clan MacLeod of Sleat. Rory Mòr MacLeod attempted to arrange a peace with Donald Gorm Mòr MacDonald.

He offered his sister, Margaret MacLeod, to Donald Gorm under an agreement, called a handfast, that allowed them to live together as man and wife for a year and a day. If Margaret bore Donald Gorm a male heir, then they would marry. If not, she would be returned to her family.

In the real story, Margaret did not bear a child at all during the appointed time and also lost sight in one of her eyes. Donald Gorm sent her back home in disgrace, tied backwards on a one-eyed horse accompanied by a one-eyed dog and a one-eyed servant.

The insult to Clan MacLeod caused a series of raids that culminated in the Battle of Coire na Creiche. The MacLeods trapped the MacDonalds in the Coire na Creiche after a MacDonald raid. The ensuing battle lasted for hours until the MacLeods were soundly defeated and thirty of them were captured. The feud didn't end until the Scottish Privy Council intervened and forced the two parties to come to a truce.

I modified the story, of course, to fit my needs. I had Aila have a baby girl named Gwyneth and used the story to signal the beginning of an all-out genocide against the Carpentini that comes to a head sixteen years later in Book III *Vengeance*.

63

FREI-OCK ISLES AND THE SOUTHLANDS

THE DEADLY JEST

A growl rumbled through the darkness.

Mara froze. Her mouth went dry.

The palpable blackness of the cave deprived her of sight, but she could still hear the approaching danger.

It was behind her, creeping quietly on padded feet, stalking her. There would be two or three of them at least. Where were the others?

Mara grasped her two fighting sticks, one in each hand, and stepped forward. These sticks had thin strips of steel set into them to make them impervious to sword strikes and yet light enough to wield. She would need that extra strength now. She carried knives strapped to her arms and waste as a back up. If it came to the knives, however, she didn't stand much of a chance.

The blood pounded in her temples, but she ignore it. Her life depended on her ability to sense the danger. To know when to strike. To avoid losing her sense of direction. Her soft leather boots made no sound as she inched her way toward the wall.

The sharp scent of wet dog reached her nostrils. She took another step. Then another.

She was close to the wall now. She could feel it in the way the air flowed about her, in the way the sounds amplified in that direction.

A claw scraped on stone. The rumbling snarl was nearer now, almost within the reach of her sticks. The creature was uncertain, or it would have rushed her by now. It couldn't see any better than she could. But it could smell her and hear her. It knew she was there.

Mara shifted her stance to face the threat, placing her back to the unseen wall. She fought to control the swooping sickness in her gut and the trembling of her hands. Any moment now.

A barking roar split the darkness.

Mara swung her sticks in a figure-eight pattern in front of her while lunging to the side. Her sticks struck twice. Wet fur brushed against her hands as the beast flew past.

It slid to a stop and scrambled back toward her.

She lunged to the side again, whirling the sticks with all the force and speed she could muster.

Two solid whacks echoed in the cavern.

The dog yelped as it fell against her knees.

Mara sprang onto its back, fumbled until she found the head of the struggling beast, slipped a stick across its throat, and clenched it tight.

The dog bucked and struggled. Mara didn't want to kill it. It wasn't the dog's fault it had been starved and sent after her, but she had no choice. The dog was driven mad with hunger and abuse. It wouldn't hesitate to tear her to shreds if it got the chance. If she let it live, it would just come after her again. Mara squeezed until the dog lay still and the twitching subsided.

"I'm sorry," she said, as she laid on hand on its damp fur and rose. The others would be coming soon. She had to get beyond their reach.

The distant slap of running feet and panting reached her. She slipped her sticks into their sheaths. Holding out one arm, she ran several steps until her hand struck solid stone. She hit the wall at an angle, scraping her knuckles, but she didn't have time to worry about that. In a few seconds, she would have more vicious, crazed dogs on top of her.

She fumbled for a handhold and realized, to her horror, that she was too short. This problem had never occurred to her. The holds had been cut for men, not for a sixteen-year old girl who stood a full head shorter than the other assassins. What had she been thinking? Few men survived the cave, and no one had attempted it at such a young age. It was too late now. She would either die today or prove that they had been wrong about her.

Mara jumped up, desperate to find some purchase on the stone.

The Deadly Jest

Her fingers slid over a hold.

She sprang again, and her fingers caught. She hauled herself up. Felt for another hold and then another. A body slammed into the wall below followed by snarling and growling. Claws scraped over stone as the dogs searched for her.

Jaws snapped closed behind her as one of the dogs leapt up. Mara curled her feet up, frantic to escape the savage, tearing fangs as she dangled precariously by one hand on a slippery hold.

Another dog growled.

She had to get out of reach of the dogs. They would be able to leap far up the wall, and she couldn't count on them missing again. She felt around with her other hand until she found a small ledge.

A dog jumped, snapping at her legs.

A tooth caught in her calf and ripped a long gash as the dog fell back to the ground.

Mara gasped and tried to ignore the searing pain and the trickle of warm blood as she pulled herself up, found a foothold, and managed to scramble onto the tiny ledge.

The dogs barked and growled beneath her. Their bodies struck the rock wall and their claws scratched the stone. The wall seemed to push against her as if it wanted to shove her down amid the snapping teeth.

Mara faced the wall and felt her way up, one agonizing hold at a time. Her forearms burned, and her injured leg trembled.

She couldn't fall.

To fall meant to die in the jaws of two starved beasts.

Her hand found the top, and she dragged herself up to straddle the wall. It was narrow at the top and dropped off sharply on the other side. She struggled to catch her breath and reached down to feel the extent of her injury. The gash didn't feel deep, but it throbbed and would weaken her calf muscle. She needed to find a way out as quickly as possible.

A tiny glimmer of light pierced the darkness—but not enough to light her way. The dogs quit barking, and she guessed they would be searching for some other way to get at her. The sound of tearing flesh and snapping bones told her they had found the body of their companion. The sour stench of bile and stomach gases from the dead dog lifted on the still air.

Mara's stomach churned in protest against the smell, and she gagged. She hadn't wanted to kill the dog, but perhaps its body would keep the others busy long enough for her to get away.

After she caught her breath, Mara let herself dangle down the backside of the wall by one hand while she searched for a hand or toehold. She didn't want to follow the wall because it led away from the light, and it certainly ended abruptly somewhere with some brutal surprise. She had to reach the light before it disappeared, or she would be left in the absolute darkness with the ravenous dogs all night. Not many who spent a night in the cave ever came out alive.

The backside of the wall was smooth. If it was the same distance to the ground as on the other side of the wall, it would only be about a fifteen foot drop, but she couldn't know that. If she let go, she could plunge to her death to be broken on the rocks below. She closed her eyes, since they weren't of use anyway, and tried to remember what Arno had taught her.

"To be an assassin," he said, "is to know fear. To live with fear. To embrace fear. Let the fear inspire you, but never let it control you."

Mara took another deep breath, stilling the pounding in her ears while trying to gather all the information she could with her other senses.

What did she hear? Between the snarling and snapping of the dogs came the quiet drip of water. What did she smell? The stink of the dead dog had dissipated to be replaced by the strong aroma of wet earth.

She pulled herself back up, found a few pieces of loose stone and tossed them away from the wall. A few seconds of silence ensued followed by the plunk of the stones breaking the surface of water.

Mara smiled. Some of the assassins had whispered about swimming in the cave when they thought no one was listening. She dropped another pebble straight down. It splashed into water. There was no way to know how deep the pool was, but the drop wasn't far. The light and her way of out the cavern was somewhere over the water. There was nothing else to do. She dangled over the wall again and let go.

The fall was farther than she had expected, but she plunged into icy cold water and came up sputtering. She searched for the tiny dot of light and settled into an easy stroke toward it. Her injured calf muscle spasmed at the cold, and she had to adjust her kick to keep it from cramping.

A splash echoed in the cavern, followed by the sound of something moving through the water on her left.

Could there be a huge, venomous snake or something equally ferocious waiting for her?

A growl rumbled over the water.

Mara cursed.

How had the dogs found her so quickly? It should have taken them more time to get around the wall.

She stroked faster. There hadn't been three dogs. There had been four. Someone had loosed a fourth dog in the tunnel on this side of the wall. Why? To make sure she failed? To kill her?

The dog made very little noise as it approached. The occasional slap of a paw on the water told her that it was close now.

Mara paused to listen.

She slipped a knife from her sheath and spun to face the quiet menace while treading water.

Sinking terror filled her stomach again, but she forced herself to remain calm. She didn't want to kill the poor animal, but if she didn't, it would latch onto her and drag her down to a watery grave.

The warmth of its breath brushed her cheek.

Its claws scraped along her chest as it paddled.

The dog snapped.

Mara threw her head back to avoid the crushing jaws and drove her knife upward into its chest. The knife stuck, so she pushed herself away from the dog and swam toward the light with a desperate flurry of strokes.

The dog floundered as if it were still trying to follow her until the haunting quiet of the darkness rushed in again. It pressed down upon her as if it wished to reduce her into the same nothingness. A pang of regret stabbed her chest. The dogs were innocent tools, and she had been forced to kill them.

Her knuckles struck stone. The jarring shock of contact sent a lightning pain up her arm. Mara dragged herself from the icy waters, trembling.

She scrambled up the rugged slope. Her calf threatened to knot up. She paused to stretch and massage it before clambering over the slippery rocks toward the point high above where the tiny light shone. That pale pinprick of light was her only hope to escape the endless night of the cavern.

She had expected a doorway or tunnel of some kind, but all she found was a hole big enough for her to poke her finger through. Her instructions had been to find the light and retrieve the diamond before the sun set. She had found the light, but how could she get through the impenetrable stone?

Mara sighed and settled on a boulder to consider. She wrapped her arms around herself to conserve some warmth and to still her violent trembling.

"An assassin has to be creative and flexible," Arno had taught her.

Mara stood and felt along the wall as far as she could reach. She pushed on the cool, damp stone. Nothing. She considered going back the way she had come rather than fail here, right on the edge of her success. But she knew she couldn't make it. She was too cold. Her fingers would never be able to grasp the stone even if she could find handholds. The suffocating blackness of the cavern would swallow her alive and never let her leave if she wandered off. She had no choice but to persist to the bitter end.

She slid her hand over the wall more slowly now, noting each crack or bump in the rock. She stopped and slid her hand back. There it was. An elongated hole wide enough for her knife blade. Like any good assassin, she always carried three or four blades on her. She retrieved the long, thin one used to find the gap in armor and inserted it into the hole. It slid in halfway and met resistance.

Mara pushed, cringing at the thought of how much filing it would take to restore the edge to her blade. A click sounded. She shoved the stone, and a door slid outward with a gravelly, scraping sound.

The blaze of warm sunlight smote her eyes and the pungent, fishy breath of moist sea air blew past her. She blinked and shaded her eyes with her hand as she peered through the opening.

Something moved.

A painful whack cracked against the top of her head.

She dropped her knife and dove through the gap. She rolled and came to her feet with her fighting sticks in her hands. Her eyes watered at the brightness of the light after the blinding darkness. A damp cave surrounded her, but the setting sun burst through the

The Deadly Jest

mouth of the cave, igniting the entire place in a dazzling light.

Master Coyne whirled from the doorway in the wall to face her. His staff swung.

She swatted it away with her sticks while ducking and sliding to the side. He didn't give her a chance to recover. Blow after blow aimed at her head or legs in an alternating pattern that gave her no chance to do more than keep the staff from striking her again.

Behind him, the huge diamond sparkled in the slanting rays of the setting sun.

He came in high.

Mara dropped to the ground, sliding toward him, feet first.

She slammed one foot into his knee, hyperextending it, before she rolled, bringing her stick up into his groin. She came to one knee and slammed the other stick behind his other knee as he bent over.

He groaned and fell face-first in the dirt. Mara leapt past him and snatched the diamond in one hand. She limped to the entrance of the cave and vaulted into the air.

"Woohoo," she cried as she plunged into the rolling sea below.

"Here are your orders," Arno said as he handed Mara the folded parchment with the black wax seal in the shape of a rook. "After you memorize them, destroy them."

Arno had a narrow, angular face with a close-cut beard and black hair. His dark eyes watched her as if he were measuring her against some ideal.

"I know the routine," Mara said.

This might be her first solo mission, but she had been on sixteen missions before. In fact, Arno had been her trainer. As a journeyman assassin, he could take on apprentices, and he had worked with Mara for the last five years.

They had traveled all over the islands and the southland since she was eleven. She had completed her apprenticeship testing in record time, and still members of the Order acted as if she couldn't take care of herself.

Members of the Order sometimes treated her as though she were incompetent. She had three marks against her before she even opened her mouth. She was young. She was female. She was small.

71

All good enough reasons for the male members of the Order to discount her—at least they thought so. Well, she had already demonstrated that they had been wrong in the testing, and now she would prove them wrong again. She was going to complete her candidacy by carrying out her first mission without any help from members of the Order.

She scanned the document. "A jester?" she said.

"He's your contact."

"Why?" she asked. Jesters had always made her uncomfortable. They had a way of seeing through you and figuring out how to humiliate you. For her, it was usually something about her size or her youthful appearance.

"Because he has access to the Duke's court," Arno explained, "and no one will take him seriously."

Mara narrowed her eyes. "Why would that be?" She could think of a dozen reasons why no one would take a jester seriously, and none of them appealed to her.

"You'll see."

Now she frowned. Arno only said "you'll see" when he wanted to hide something from her.

"I don't need any more unpleasant surprises," Mara said. "Like that fourth dog you sent in there to kill me."

Arno shook his head. "I didn't send the fourth dog," he said. "The masters did. And the jester's not unpleasant, but I don't want to prejudice your opinion."

"In other words," Mara corrected him, "he's a real handful, and you want me to figure things out on my own."

Arno smiled. Then he laid a hand on Mara's shoulder and looked down at her. He was imposing at over six feet tall, whereas she was barely five feet. His hand felt heavy on her shoulder, and his gaze took on that fatherly expression he sometimes had.

"You know I trust you," he said. "This may not appear to be a hazardous mission, but things can get out of hand quickly. Keep your weapons on you at all times, trust no one, and don't be afraid to disengage if it gets too dangerous."

"I'm only stealing a letter long enough to copy it," Mara said with a glance down at her orders. "How hard can it be?"

"It's not just any letter," Arno explained. "We think it contains

The Deadly Jest

details about an alliance between King Tristan of the Dunkeldi and King Rupert of the Hallstat. They might be planning to invade Coll."

"Okay," Mara said with a shrug of her shoulders.

"People will kill to keep that kind of information secret," Arno said.

"I understand." She had already been fighting the nervous butterflies in her stomach, and now he had to go and say something like that.

The Order of the Rook kept track of what was happening in all the isles and the mainlands that bordered the Alborian Sea. They sold information and eliminated uncooperative and dangerous opponents—all for the purpose of maintaining peace and stability. Of course, they charged for their services. Hidden away in their stronghold on the Black Isle of Nairn, they had become the power behind many a throne.

Mara had been on missions like this before with Arno, but he had always had her back. This time she was alone. If she messed up, no one was going to be there to pick up the pieces.

Arno tapped the parchment with the orders. "They can't know that you have secured the letter. Make a copy as quickly as you can and put it back."

"I read the orders," Mara said. She didn't want him to know how nervous she was, and it annoyed her that Arno might think she was too simple to understand and follow instructions. She had done fine in the caves, better than anyone before her, in fact.

Arno pulled her into a hug.

"I'm sorry, little one," he said. "It's just hard for me to let you go."

Mara squeezed him back, blinking at the sting of tears. Arno had been like a father to her since he had snatched her from the burning ruins of some castle on Perth. Of all the people in the Order she knew and respected, she loved Arno more than all of them combined. Everything she knew about staying alive she owed to him.

She cleared her throat. "I'm a big girl," she said.

Arno smiled down at her with raised eyebrows as if to say no girl barely five feet tall could call herself big.

"I know," he said. "Remember that you are only a candidate. The masters of the Order are still testing you. Be careful. Be efficient. Get the information. That's all you have to do."

"And stay alive while I'm doing it."

"That too," Arno said.

Mara clung to the shadows of an empty stall on the edge of the marketplace in the city of Kirn. Criers hawked their wares. Buyers haggled over prices. The rich aroma of baking bread and roasting meat competed with the odor of rotting filth from the street. Mara wrapped her mottled cloak about her despite the heat as she studied the folk that passed through the gates of Castle Kirn.

The curtain walls of the castle pushed against the town. The castle occupied one of the seven hills that made up Kirn. The jagged teeth of the Kirn Mountains rose behind it, overshadowing the entire town. One round tower and one square tower flanked the gate where the fangs of the portcullis poised overhead.

A bridge spanned the dry moat that surrounded the castle. The walls stood forty feet high, topped with alternating embrasures and merlons with arrow slits in them. Mara had already found the weak spot in the castle layout and construction. Now she settled in to watch the passersby.

Those that entered the castle varied from wealthy courtiers to poor peasant folk. Couriers rode in and out, and people of fashion and wealth made a display of visiting the castle. Two women in particular drew her attention. One was a thin, quiet young lady with piercing blue eyes. She rode her horse sidesaddle and held her head high, but she nodded to the guards, and once, Mara heard her thank a man who stepped out of her way.

The other woman wore a bright blue dress and had a round, jovial face that she hung out of her sedan chair carried by two sweating men.

"Walk faster, can't you?" she demanded in a voice that carried over half the market square.

The contrast between them drew Mara's attention. Who were they?

For two days, she had studied the castle, noting the movement of the guards, how many there were, and when they changed. She had examined the wall for defects in construction and design that would allow her to enter unobserved. Few noticed her presence in the shadows of the empty stall. Those that did edged away from her.

The Deadly Jest

A shabby dog nosed around her feet, but she shooed it away.

Mara waited for the comforting cover of nightfall as the bustle of the market quieted and the merchants shut up their shops. Patrons deserted the streets, leaving them to the waifs and misfits for whom Hallstat society had no place. A few ragged boys and girls scampered about, rummaging through the trash.

A mother passed, carrying an infant in one arm and towing a toddler behind her with the other. Mara watched her with that peculiar feeling of loss she often had when she saw mothers with their children. She had never known her own mother. The Order had been her only family. Arno, the masters, the other spies and assassins had been father figures and brothers. But Mara had never known the tender touch of a mother's hand.

No mother had ever sung her to sleep or told her bedtime stories. No mother had ever held her hand or instructed her in what it meant to be a woman. Mara tried to swallow the knot that rose in her throat and blinked at the burning tears in her eyes. Why couldn't she be rational when it came to mothers and children?

Mara shook herself from the moment of weakness and stole from her hiding place, crossed the road, and slid down the slope into the dry moat that surrounded the castle. She worked her way up to the corner of the round tower where the plaster had not been so skillfully applied. The thin coat crumbled and peeled off easily. Mara drew the file from her cloak and worked it into the cracks between the stones to scrape out the mortar. The bitter taste of lime from the mortar dusted her tongue.

Once she had several hand and toeholds cleared as high as she could reach, she began her ascent. It was tedious, dangerous work, but she thrilled at the challenge. There was nothing so freeing as being suspended between earth and sky, defying the boundaries of human weakness. She had been the best climber in the Order for years now. Still, she knew better than to trust the stones set in castle walls. She tested each one to make sure it was secure before trusting her weight on it. Loose stones would mean a certain fall and serious injury or death.

She worked methodically, scraping out new handholds, working her way up a few feet at a time. The scuffing of footfalls on the walkway above forced her to pause, hugging close to the wall, the rough plaster scratching her cheek. A guard would only see her if he looked straight down the wall, which he was unlikely to do. When the footsteps retreated, Mara finished the climb, checked to make sure the walkway was clear, and then scrambled through an embrasure.

The exercise had been invigorating. She hadn't had much chance for exercise in the two and half weeks it had taken her to sail from the isle of Nairn to Royan and then by horse across the rolling plain country of Kirn to the castle town on the southern flanks of the Kirn Mountains. Mara crouched and skulked along the walkway until she could descend the stairs and dodge into the deeper shadows of a storage shed.

"It took you long enough," a voice whispered from out of the darkness.

Mara drew a knife and crouched, ready for action. A short young man with a bald head stepped out of the shadows, smiling at her. He wore a loose tunic secured with a belt at his waist and tight trousers that he tucked into his boots. The clothes accentuated his muscular physique and a pleasant, almost handsome face. He couldn't have been more than sixteen. The boy extended a hand.

"Muckle Jack," he said.

Mara glanced at the hand and scowled.

"What kind of name is that?"

"I'm a jester," he said with a big grin.

"Are you funny?" Mara asked. She couldn't help it. Every jester she had met had been a bore.

Muckle Jack made a funny face and wiggled his ears. "Of course," he said.

"Where are your weird clothes?"

Muckle Jack smirked. "I don't wear them all the time, only when I'm working."

"Right. Okay," Mara said, "how did you know I would come in here?"

"I've been watching you," he replied.

"From where?" Mara asked in surprise. It disturbed her that she hadn't noticed anyone watching her, that she hadn't felt his gaze.

"Up there." He pointed to a tall building that overlooked the walls. "You're not the only one who can climb."

Mara harrumphed. "Let's go," she said.

The Deadly Jest

This wasn't what she had expected, though she noted with considerable satisfaction that Muckle Jack was shorter than her by at least an inch, even though he looked to be about her age. He disappeared into the shadows, and she followed.

They passed between rows of thatched cottages and over the cobblestone streets, between a long row of two-story barracks to a building with chimneys so tall that Mara couldn't see the tops of them in the dark. Candlelight flickered in windows as they passed, and the sounds of laughter and human voices filtered into the streets.

Jack finally ducked into a building near the kitchens. He lit a candle as she entered the small room. The yellow flame flickered, casting a pale light over a water pump that stood in the center of the room and dozens of buckets and barrels that lined the shelves and walls. The stone floor was damp.

"Why didn't you just come in the gate earlier?" Jack asked. "It would have been easier."

"Because I didn't want to be seen," Mara said as she folded her arms.

Jack smiled. "Or were you just trying to show off?"

"Drop it," Mara said. "Let's just get to work."

"Suit yourself," Jack said. "But, if you insist on doing things the hard way, you might be here awhile."

This kid was exasperating. No wonder Arno wouldn't tell her about him. She might not have come.

"So, what's your plan?" Mara asked. "I was told you could give me access to the Duke's study and personal chambers."

"I can get you access to anything," Jack said. He gave her a broad grin.

Mara simply gazed at him, waiting for him to continue.

Jack set the candle on top of a barrel and rummaged in a bin. Mara noted the knots of muscles in his neck and forearms and his broad shoulders. For being such a short, irritating fellow, Jack looked powerful—not someone to be underestimated. Jack held out a bundle of clothes.

"You'll need to put these on," he said, shoving the bundle into her arms.

Mara scowled. One was clearly a dress, and there were few things Mara hated more than dresses. She had grown up wearing trousers and roaming the rocky slopes of Nairn Isle, training in combat, tracking, and hunting. She only wore a dress when she had to go undercover with Arno.

Jack stood taller and puffed out his chest. "I've arranged with the cook for you to be the new ewery maid of the west wing."

"The what?"

"You know," Jack said. "You see to the drinking and washing water at the tables in the great hall during meals and in all the rooms of the west wing."

Mara hadn't planned on being a maid. How would she have time to search for the letter? Mara turned the bundle of clothes over. Jack smirked at her.

"What? You think you're better than the rest of us because you get to wear a cloak and run around with a black rook in your pocket?"

"Keep quiet," Mara snapped. "Someone might hear you."

"Well," Jack continued, "I had to collect a lot of favors to get this position for you. The least you could do is say thanks."

"Right. Thanks," Mara said. "Does the cook know who I am?"

Jack rammed his hands onto his hips. "Of course not. How stupid do you think I am?"

Something about the way he said this made Mara study him. "What aren't you telling me?" she said.

"Well," Jack glanced at the ground and shuffled his feet, "I might have told him that you and I are betrothed."

Mara resisted the urge to reach out and throttle him. "You *might* have told him?" she repeated with exaggerated calm.

"Don't get your smock all in a twist," Jack said as he waved away her concern with a dismissive flick of the wrist. "I've been telling him for years that I had a girl out there to keep him from forcing me to court his ugly niece." He shivered, but then his gaze ran over Mara. "You're definitely a step up from any of the cook's relatives."

"Don't get any ideas," Mara said. "Remember that I've killed people for less."

Jack wouldn't stop smiling, which made her clench her jaw.

"Look," Jack said. "If you want to get into the Duke's rooms, this is the best way to do it without causing suspicion. But I warn you, Duke Peyton is supposed to leave in a couple of days, and, if you don't find whatever you're looking for soon, you might not get the chance."

Mara considered the bundle. She didn't have any other option, so she set the clothes on a barrel and lifted a long strap of linen from the pile.

"What am I supposed to do with this?" she asked.

Jack wiggled his ears again. "They only told me they were sending a woman. I didn't know how big you'd be, so I got a wrap or this." He pulled out an oddly-shaped piece of cloth with two sacks.

"What the heck is that?" Mara demanded.

Jack grinned, and his gaze strayed to Mara's chest. "You know. The cook's wife called it a breast bag. The bigger ladies use them."

"Get out," Mara said, and she snatched the undergarment from his hands.

Jack laughed. "I've got to get changed anyway. Meet me over by the big doors. I'll introduce you to the cook, and you can start tonight."

The delicious aroma of roasting meat wafted out of the kitchen as Mara waited in the darkness for Muckle Jack to arrive. She was already sweating under the heavy linen dress. The wraps pinched her chest, but there was no way she would be caught dead or alive with those breast bags on. The very idea turned her stomach. Better to have a flat chest than to stuff yourself in a bag. She wasn't big enough to need that kind of support anyway.

Mara reached down to scratch at the hose and garters. She had forgotten what it was like to be a woman out in the real world. Unless they wanted to tell her she couldn't do something, everyone in the Order treated her like anybody else. She was allowed to dress as a man because the volumes of underclothing and long dresses women had to wear made it impossible to do much of what an assassin needed to do.

It had taken some time to adjust her knives so they were accessible without being visible. She strapped one to her thigh and one to each arm under the long sleeves of the dress. The thin leather slippers weren't nearly as comfortable as her boots, and the fabric hairnet kept trying to slide off her head because she didn't have long enough hair to hold it up. The bright blue and white colors of the dress made her feel exposed. She much preferred the anonymity of a dark cloak.

Jack sauntered toward her with a rhythmic jingle. He wore tight hose and a fitted silk shirt. Each leg of the hose was a different color—one bright red and the other yellow. The silk shirt bore a checkered pattern of purple and green. On his head, he had strapped a huge pair of donkey ears by tying them under his chin. Each ear had a little bell hanging from it.

"You look ridiculous," Mara said.

"That is the point," Jack said. "And you look uncomfortable."

"I am."

"Well, don't show it," Jack said. "They'll think I'm courting a simpleton."

Mara smirked, but he ignored her.

"The cook's in here."

Jack pushed through the doors, and Mara followed.

She tried not to gape at the size of the kitchen or at the two dozen people scurrying about. A tall, thin man with a bright red face and a white cap on his head caught sight of them and waded through the chaos to greet them.

"Ah," he said as he bent to peer at Mara. "Muckle, my friend. I had no idea your lady love was so beautiful. Now I see why your head could not be turned."

Mara smiled sweetly and reached a foot over to step on Jack's toes, wishing she could grind them into the stone floor.

"Well, well," the cook said. "Have you any experience waiting at tables?"

"No sir," Mara said.

The cook puckered his lips. "Hmm. Well then, we'll start you with the wash basins."

He snapped his fingers. "Sarah," he called. A young woman, maybe a year or two older than Mara, hurried over to them. "Take Mara and instruct her in the wash basins." He winked at Mara and Jack. "She is a special friend of Muckle Jack."

Sarah gave Mara a restrained smile and led her to where several other girls were filling pitchers. Sarah was a plump young woman with an open, pleasing face. A wisp of dark hair poked from under her cap. She flipped a towel over Mara's arm and handed her a porcelain bowl half-filled with water.

"Wait until I call you," she said. "Don't splash on anyone, keep your gaze down and your mouth shut. You are not to be seen or heard. Is that clear?"

"Yes, miss," Mara said, trying to be as submissive as she could, though it was a real challenge. Growing up in the heart of an order of assassins did not reward submissiveness.

Sarah waved a hand. "Wait by the door and stay out of the way."

Mara tripped over to stand by the door, struggling to keep the dress from getting underfoot.

Jack came up to stand beside her as she peered through the doorway into the great hall. Several rows of long tables stood perpendicular to a high table at the far end of the room. Lords and ladies decked out in their finery filtered in to find seats.

"That's Lord Peyton, the Duke of Kirn," Jack whispered, pointing to the long table. "The one just stepping up to the high table."

"He's not much older than we are," Mara observed. The Duke was slender and wore a loose-fitting, blue tunic, white silk trousers, and high black boots. He tied his dark hair back with a thin ribbon.

"He's already twenty-one," Jack said. "He just looks young for his age."

The two ladies Mara had seen entering the castle earlier in the day came in from different sides of the room. "Who are they?" she asked.

Jack chuckled. "The big one is Lady Erica, daughter of the Duke of Einbeck. She's desperate to win Duke Peyton's hand in marriage."

Mara looked over at Jack. "Does he like her?" She couldn't see what would be attractive about such a loudmouth lady, but she didn't understand these things.

"I don't know."

"So who's the thin one?"

"She's Lady Alicia, daughter of the Earl of Mayen. She's the friend of Lady Thea, the Duke's sister. I heard that Lady Thea wanted them to marry, but Duke Peyton's father always insisted on nothing less than a foreign princess or a Duke's daughter. The princess of Kassan was here last summer before Duke Peyton's father died. Man, was she a real eye catcher."

"Is Lady Alicia after the Duke, too, then?" Mara asked.

"I don't think so," Jack said. "She's just here to visit Lady Thea. She comes every spring."

"Which one is Lady Thea?"

Jack pointed. "She's the one with the red hat and white lace hairnet."

Mara noted that Lady Thea was a plain-looking young woman with dark hair. She might be in her late teens.

"The man with the blue cape is Duke Peyton's steward," Jack said. "He's called Lord Dain. I would avoid serving him if you can, though. He can get handsy." Jack wiggled his eyebrows at her.

"Thanks for the warning," Mara said.

The servers, bearing trays of bread and cheese and huge platters of roasted venison and fowl, swept past them.

"Well. You're on your own now," Jack said. "I've got to prepare my steed for battle." He left her, and Mara gazed after him. Would he be riding a horse into the great hall during dinner?

Sarah stepped over, bearing a white, clay pitcher.

"Follow me," she said.

They entered the great hall, and Mara couldn't help but gaze up at the huge chandelier with more than a hundred candles burning overhead and the giant tapestries that covered the walls. The wooden beams of the ceiling were shaped like the hull of a ship. It was a grand sight.

Sarah stopped her. "You wait by the door and watch the others," she said. "When I signal to you, approach the lords and ladies who have finished on their left. Always on their left. If they ignore you, bow and move to the next one. If they accept, you hold the basin so that they can wash, and wait while they dry their hands on the towel. Got it?"

"Yes," Mara said. How hard could it be?

"When the water and towel are soiled," Sarah continued, "you return here for a clean one."

Sarah waited for her to nod and then scurried off to fill cups with amber-colored mead.

The noise of the hall grew louder as the meal progressed. Above it all, the voice of Lady Erica reigned supreme. Mara caught Duke Peyton looking at Lady Erica several times. She couldn't decide what his expression meant. The Duke was a lean, handsome young man who didn't talk much to those around him. He had dark hair, like most of the Hallstat, and a long nose.

"Are you waiting for a personal invitation?"

Mara jerked her head around. Sarah glared at her with her hands on her hips. "They've already finished with the meat," she said. "Go. Go." Sarah shooed her toward the table.

Mara hurried across the floor, nearly tripping over her dress. She approached an old man who appeared to be finished and was holding up his greasy hands. When she slid in beside him, he glanced up at her and paused.

"Oh, my pretty," he said. "I haven't had the pleasure of seeing you before."

Mara cringed at the disgusting old man, but kept her gaze on the table. If he tried anything, she would maim him for the rest of his life.

The man dipped his hands in the water and wiped them on the towel before tossing it back over her arm. She bowed and tried to leave, when his hand grabbed her elbow. Her first instinct was to roll her elbow down in a savage strike to his collarbone, but she held still, refusing to meet his gaze.

"Look at me," he said.

"My Lord?" she questioned without taking her gaze from the table.

"I said look at me," he demanded again.

Mara raised her gaze and found him studying her with interest. He glanced around the room and leaned toward her. "You're no servant girl," he said.

"I'm new," Mara said, trying to appear as sheepish and submissive as possible.

The man grunted. "You're too pretty to be a servant anyway," he said. "I'm going to speak to the Duke about you."

"Please, no," Mara said.

Now the man scowled at her. He had a scheming expression on his face. She didn't trust him.

"Why not?" he asked.

"Because I just started, and I need this job," Mara said. "I don't want any trouble."

"Hmm," the man said. "I'll be watching you." He released her elbow, and she rushed to the next noble.

She had gone back to the kitchen for clean water twice when the music of flutes and drums burst through the hall. She paused and looked up. Muckle Jack rode in on the back of an enormous hound with his donkey ears flapping and jingling. He looked so ridiculous that she couldn't help but smile.

Jack did a handstand on the dog's back, then resumed his seat and began juggling a dozen balls as the dog padded around the room. A scattering of applause came from the tables as lords and ladies adjusted to watch the performance. Jack caught a ball in his mouth and balanced another on his head as he kept the other balls going. Then he slid from the dog's back, executed several back handsprings before he launched into a double flip, landed, and fell into a split. The dog padded up and licked his face.

The audience laughed and applauded.

"Give us a riddle, fool," a man shouted.

Mara noted the scowl that crossed Jack's face. Apparently, he didn't like being called a fool. She glanced around. A knight dressed in a red tunic smiled, apparently pleased that he had called the attention of the gathering to himself. He appeared to be in his mid-twenties and had a huge nose that was as wide as it was long.

Jack rolled out of the splits, cartwheeled, and somersaulted until he stood facing the knight.

"Your life can be measured in hours," Jack said. A murmur swept through the crowd as the hall became quiet. "You serve by being devoured. Thin, you are quick. Fat, you are slow. Wind is your foe. What are you?"

The knight frowned, trying to decide whether Jack had insulted him or not.

"Shall I repeat the riddle for this valiant knight of the nose?" Jack called out.

Laughter rippled through the crowd, but the knight did not smile. Mara worried that Jack might go too far and get himself into trouble.

"Perhaps his wits have taken refuge beneath his copious beak and are afraid to come out and play."

The lady sitting next to the knight laid a hand on his arm as if to restrain him while the rest of the crowd laughed, clearly enjoying Jack's performance. Mara stepped away from the table in case trou-

The Deadly Jest

ble erupted.

"Who is the fool now?" Jack said. He did a back handspring and climbed onto the dog's back.

"Speak for him, Mutton," Jack said.

The dog barked a deep resonating woof that echoed throughout the hall.

"Our valiant knight has lost his tongue," Jack said.

The dog barked again, while Jack started juggling.

"Can no one help our poor, deformed friend?" Jack cried, throwing the balls higher and higher.

The knight lunged to his feet and threw a goblet at Jack, who dodged the missile, but the red wine splashed across his silk shirt. He let the balls drop to the ground as a hush settled over the hall.

"Watch your words, my fine, foolish dwarf," the knight said, "or I will pound a few inches off your height."

Mara tried to decide if she should draw her knives and go to Jack's defense.

Jack jumped from the dog's back and strode up to the knight. He craned his head back, exaggerating the movement, to glare up at him. The donkey ears flapped comically, but no one laughed. Jack stood a full foot and a half shorter than the knight.

"The answer to the riddle," Jack said, "is a candle. But dimwits whose brains reside in their snouts can hardly be expected to solve a child's conundrum."

The knight's face burned red, and he raised a hand as if he meant to strike. Jack reached up and tweaked his nose. The knight lunged after him, but Jack did several back handsprings to avoid him. Then he stood with his hands on his hips and wiggled his donkey ears. The bells tinkled in the quiet hall.

"Which is the bigger ass?" Jack said. "The one who flees or the one who pursues?"

Laughter rippled through the gathering, who were clearly growing more uneasy with the exchange. Mara had seen this kind of thing before. The jester's job was to poke fun at the silliness of their society and at human foibles, but not everyone had the personality to endure such public scorn.

The knight tried to grab Jack, but Jack slipped between his legs and swept the man's feet from underneath him as he did. Then he rolled away and did a few somersaults before he faced the knight, who had fallen to his knees.

"I think that's enough, Muckle," Duke Peyton called from the high table.

Muckle Jack faced him and did a dramatic bow with a sweep of his hand. The knight came to his feet.

"I demand satisfaction," the knight said.

Duke Peyton rose, resting his hands on the table. "You provoked the jester," he said. "If you don't like the way he plays then find your seat and let the rest of us enjoy the performance."

"I demand satisfaction," the knight said again.

"What would you have me do?" Duke Peyton demanded. "Put you both in the ring?"

Jack bowed again. "I will happily meet this knave of a knight with the monstrous nose on any field of battle."

"Why you—" the knight began.

Jack wiggled the ears at him again. "If you can't take the jest, you shouldn't come to the party," he said.

"I don't want my jester injured," Duke Peyton said.

"Me?" Jack exclaimed, placing a hand on his chest as if the very idea were nonsense.

"Quiet, Muck," Duke Peyton ordered. Then he sighed. "All right. If you two insist, then you will duel at first light tomorrow. The one to draw the first blood wins, and the other will apologize."

Jack grinned and bowed to the knight. "On the morrow," he said, "we will discover who the true fool is." Then he bounded to the dog, climbed onto his back, and rode out of the great hall.

"What's the matter with you?" Mara demanded as Jack led her to her new quarters after she had helped clear the great hall. They had passed the pump room so she could retrieve her other clothes.

Jack made a face at her.

"You baited that knight to attack you."

"That's my job," Jack said. "I'm supposed to tell jokes, insult people, make a mockery of our society and people's arrogance. That's what jesters do."

"You humiliated him."

The Deadly Jest

"It's all in good fun," Jack said. "Some cowards just can't take it."

Mara shook her head. "Eventually, you're going to pick the wrong man and get yourself killed."

Now Jack scowled. "Why is it that because I'm small everyone assumes I can't do anything?" His gaze passed over Mara. "I assumed someone like you would know better."

Mara stared at him. He was right. That's what everyone in the Order did to her. Men were constantly telling her that she couldn't do things because she was a woman and because she was small.

"Sorry," she said. "But you can't get yourself killed. You're my only contact."

Jack smirked at her. "Thanks for being concerned about my welfare."

"You know what I mean."

"Do I?" Jack said.

Mara clicked her tongue. "What weapon will you choose?" she asked. "Do you even know how to fight?"

Jack smiled. "You'll see," he said as he stopped beside a door under a set of stairs. "I got you a room to yourself," he said, "so you wouldn't have to deal with the other maids' prying eyes."

"Thanks," Mara said. "You think of everything."

"That's why I'm so valuable." He grinned. "How about giving your betrothed a goodnight kiss?"

Mara raised a hand to strike him, flexed her fist, and smiled.

"Don't try my patience," she said and lifted the latch. Then she stopped. "You're not going to get killed tomorrow, are you?" she asked.

Jack smirked, and Mara raised her hands to fend off his anger.

"All right. It's just that I need you to tell me everything you know about where the Duke keeps important items."

"Like what?"

"I can't tell you that," she said.

Jack puckered his lips and blew her a kiss. "Goodnight my fairy goddess," he said. "I will dream of the sultry tones of your sweet voice and the caress of your gentle hand."

Mara rolled her eyes and stepped into her room.

It was small—nothing more than a cupboard with a tiny bed and wash basin. She dropped her clothes and weapons on the bed, shoved them aside, and fell onto it. She didn't have the energy to do more than stare up into the darkness. She needed to find the letter tomorrow, with or without Jack. If the Duke was leaving in a few days, then he might take the letter with him and deliver it to the King. If that happened, this assignment would become very complicated.

The next morning, Mara gazed out over the courtyard where fresh sand had been spread in preparation for the duel. A ring had been roped off and benches erected. A raised dais with a canopy held several chairs and a table. The two ladies visiting the Duke were already seated on opposite ends of the dais. Lady Erica chatted loudly with the young man seated next to her. Lady Alicia sat beside Lady Thea conversing in low tones. The Duke's green banner with its white tree flapped over the pavilion. The air was already warm with the promise of a hot day. Mara noted that the white-haired man who had accosted her the day before was nowhere to be seen.

Sarah had guided Mara to the arena as the entire court and the servants turned out to see the spectacle. Apparently, morning chores could wait. Sarah pushed her way to the front of the roped off area and stood twisting a kerchief around her fingers. Mara studied her for a moment, realizing for the first time that Sarah probably liked Jack. Mara could see why. He was strong, funny, and good-looking—despite his bald head.

"You think he has a chance?" Mara asked.

Sarah glowered at her. "I thought you were betrothed," she snapped. "Honestly, you act as if you don't know him."

"Uh, well, we haven't been—" Mara scrambled to come up with an explanation, but a cheer rose from the crowd as Jack came riding out, seated on his great hound.

He wore no helmet or mail, only a simple linen gambeson and leather gloves. At least this time he hadn't tied on the donkey ears. He had a lot nerve. For him, this was probably just another performance.

The knight strode out after him, sporting a shining steel helmet with a noseguard and a full mail hauberk that fell to his thighs. He also wore plate gauntlets covering his hands and greaves upon his shins. In truth, he had left little exposed from which Jack could draw

The Deadly Jest

blood.

A few boos followed the knight's entrance. Jack was clearly the crowd's favorite, but his refusal to equip himself with proper armor made it seem as if he were trying to give the knight every advantage he could.

Duke Peyton climbed the dais, nodded to the ladies, and sat at a table. "To the center," he called.

Jack dropped to the ground and did a backflip before he strode to meet the knight. Someone ran to usher the dog out.

"Since Lord Doran of Cassel has issued this challenge," Duke Peyton said, "Muckle Jack will choose the weapon."

"Longsword," Jack shouted. A murmur ran through the crowd. Duke Peyton shook his head as if he understood what Jack was doing and disapproved. Mara glanced at Sarah.

"Has he ever fought with a longsword?" she asked, forgetting that she was supposedly well-acquainted with Jack.

Sarah shrugged and continued to twist the kerchief around her fingers.

Two men, also wearing mail hauberks, entered the ring carrying longswords. When one of them handed the sword to Jack, he made a show of struggling to handle it, earning a ripple of laughter and applause from the crowd. The sword was almost as tall as he was.

Lord Doran hefted his longsword in both hands and assumed a fighting stance.

"Remember," Duke Peyton said, "this is not a fight to the death. Men are on hand to prevent things from going too far. The first to draw blood will withdraw to allow an inspection of the injury, and the first to bleed agrees to concede the fight. Any questions?"

They both shook their heads.

"When the flag falls, you may begin."

Duke Peyton held out a red kerchief. Jack had stabbed the longsword into the sand and leaned on the pommel and handguard as if he didn't have a care in the world. He should have been frightened. One solid strike with a longsword, and Jack could be permanently injured or even killed. Mara's heartbeat quickened and sweat beaded on her brow.

Duke Peyton dropped the flag.

Lord Doran lunged, swinging the blade in a wide arc at Jack's head.

Jack ducked and drove a foot directly into Lord Doran's knee.

Lord Doran stumbled and staggered back, favoring the leg. Jack rose to lean on the sword.

Mara couldn't help but be impressed. She used that same technique. Knees were a useful weak spot—especially for tall people who always thought they had the height and reach advantage.

Lord Doran brought the longsword down in a terrible stroke that might have cleaved Jack in two.

Jack snapped his longsword up with a strength and speed that surprised Mara and deflected the stroke into the sand.

Then he swung his foot up and slammed it into Lord Doran's exposed elbow.

Lord Doran roared in pain and backed away.

Jack resumed leaning on his sword.

"I'm ready when you are," he said. The crowd hooted with pleasure.

Mara smiled at his brazenness. He wasn't trying to defeat Lord Doran. He was trying to permanently humiliate him.

Lord Doran charged, swinging the longsword in a flurry.

Jack met each stroke as he scuttled backwards.

The clang of steel on steel echoed in the courtyard.

Jack slipped inside the reach of Lord Doran's longsword, flipped his sword around, and slammed the pommel into Lord Doran's face.

The nosepiece of his helmet bent inward, and blood gushed from his nose.

Jack whirled away and slapped Lord Doran on the backside with the flat of his sword.

The crowd roared and lunged to their feet with wild applause.

Mara shook her head. Jack was completely insane. He couldn't resist the temptation to perform for the crowd.

A cry of warning escaped Mara's throat, and a gasp burst from the crowd as Lord Doran roared and rushed Jack. The sword swung in a powerful horizontal arc as if Lord Doran intended to cut Jack in two. Jack leapt into the air and somersaulted over the sword.

"Foul!" the crowd shouted as Jack landed and rolled before coming to his feet with the sword in front of him. Two men rushed in to restrain Lord Doran, who ripped off his helmet and spat blood.

"I'll kill you," he shouted.

The Deadly Jest

"Get him out of here," Duke Peyton called. "If you ever set foot on my lands again, Lord Doran, I'll have you thrown in chains."

"Behold, the bleeding beak," Jack shouted. He held the longsword aloft as the men escorted Lord Doran out of the courtyard. The crowd cheered and applauded.

Duke Peyton leapt over the barrier and strode up to Jack, shaking his head.

"One of these days," he said, "you're going to go too far."

Jack grinned. "A man does good business who rids himself of a turd," he said in a loud voice that carried. Duke Peyton tried to cover a smile and walked away.

Mara watched as the crowd dispersed, heading back to their duties. She followed them when a thought struck her. How could she be so stupid? This would have been the perfect time to search the Duke's quarters when everyone in the castle was distracted. Instead, she had allowed herself to be caught up in the show Jack was putting on to entertain the court. She had even found herself anxious for his welfare.

By noon, Mara despaired that she would ever get enough time alone to search for the letter. Sarah had led her through the two dozen rooms of the west wing and shown her where all the ewery closets were and how to move unseen by the occupants of the castle. A series of back-stairs and hallways allowed the servants to pass quickly from one part of the castle to another without ever having to intrude into the private space of the lords and ladies.

After the first hour, Mara became acutely aware of the bruises the heavy water buckets had rubbed on her legs. She was accustomed to strenuous exercise, but the constant weight of the water buckets banging against her thighs and ankles and jerking at her shoulders was beginning to wear.

"This study is off limits," Sarah explained as she showed Mara the Duke's quarters. She pointed to a heavy oak door with a lock on it. "If you go in there, you will be dismissed."

Mara didn't bother to point out the lock. She knew how to pick locks, of course, but it was comical that Sarah would think a ewery maid capable of walking through locked doors.

"Doesn't he need water in there?" Mara asked.

Sarah clicked her tongue disapprovingly. "Around here, you do not ask questions. You simply do as you are told."

Mara considered the locked study. That must be where the Duke had hidden the letter.

That afternoon, Mara rushed through the other rooms, filling pitchers and emptying and cleaning the wash basins as quickly as she could. Duke Peyton had gone hunting with some of the nobles, and she knew his quarters would be deserted.

She slipped into his room with its high bed and polished wooden desk and began a systematic search of the room. She checked every slot in the desk. Searched under the bed. Lifted the mattress. Flipped through the books. Squeezed the tassels on the curtains for any rolled up pieces of paper. Checked the clothes in the wardrobe. Looked behind the tapestry that hung on the wall. Lifted the woolen rugs. Tapped on the floor and walls in search of a secret hiding place. Nothing.

When she had finished, she stood in the middle of the room with her hands on her hips, trying to think of where she had missed. She stared at the solid oak door that led to the Duke's private study. It had to be in there. She lifted the bucket to finish her chores. Perhaps she had been naïve, but she had hoped that finding the letter would be fairly straightforward. It was just a piece of paper, after all.

She finished her chores as the sun dropped low in the horizon. Then she hurried to the kitchen, wondering where Jack had been all day. He met her before she reached the kitchen and pulled her into a narrow alcove so that their bodies were pressed together. Mara shoved him farther into the alcove to make more room.

"Did you find it?" Jack questioned.

Mara shook her head. "It's got to be in his study. I'm going in there tonight."

"That's risky," Jack said. "He'll probably be back by then, and he'll hear you."

"Now who's assuming someone can't do something?" Mara teased.

"I never said you couldn't do it," Jack said, raising his hands in surrender. "Just that it's risky."

Mara glanced at Jack's clothes. He wore his simple tunic and tight hose. "Aren't you performing tonight?"

The Deadly Jest

"No," Jack said. "When the Duke's out, I don't usually perform. Besides, Lord Peyton told me to take a break. He said I was a bit too insulting last night."

"No," Mara said in feigned shock.

"I know," Jack said. "He pays me to tease and insult people, and then he gets grumpy when he finds out that I'm good at it."

"You're very modest," Mara said.

He grinned. The sound of footsteps approached, and Jack grabbed Mara and pulled her into a kiss. The move so stunned Mara that she froze for an instant before she punched him in the gut. He grunted and let go of her.

"What do you think you're doing?" Mara demanded.

"It's part of the disguise," Jack said. "If people see us conversing in private and we don't look like we're courting, they'll start to talk. It could blow your cover."

Mara ground her teeth. He had a point, but he should have asked first.

"You do that again," she said, "and I'll rip those lips off your face and stuff them up your nose."

Laughter played across Jack's face as he tried not to make too much noise.

"For a spy," he said, "you don't play your part very well."

"You chose this disguise for me," she protested.

"It's a good one, if you don't ruin it," Jack said.

Mara stared at him. What was wrong with her? She usually had more control and confidence.

"I'm sorry," she said.

Jack waved a dismissive hand at her. "You're going to be late," he said. "I'll find you after dinner and show you how to get into Duke Peyton's study."

"I can get in on my own," Mara said. She wasn't about to forgive him for kissing her, though she had been surprised at how pleasant it was.

The white-haired man watched her throughout the evening meal, and Mara was glad to escape the noise and sneers of the lords and ladies when the meal was finished and the hall had been cleaned. She slipped into her normal clothes and stole out of the castle to circle around to the west wing, keeping to the shadows, trusting her mottled cloak to keep her from being seen. Duke Peyton's rooms were on the second floor. His windows remained dark. This meant that he hadn't yet returned from the hunt. Mara found this odd but wasn't going to waste the chance.

Fortunately, the walls of the inner buildings hadn't been plastered. It would be an easy matter to reach the second floor. The problem would be forcing the window. Mara prepared herself and climbed. She tested each handhold before trusting her weight to it. The west wing had been well-built, and she reached the window in a few minutes. She pushed on it, but it didn't give.

She withdrew a thin piece of metal from her pocket and slipped it into the crack, sliding it up in search of the latch. When the blade made contact with the latch, Mara pushed on it to lift it free. The piece of metal popped out as if it had been shoved.

Mara nearly fell from the wall in surprise, trying to understand how and why the latch had done that. Did it have a spring on it to prevent it from being forced? She slipped the metal in again, and the same thing happened. Mara replaced the piece of metal in her pocket and clung to the wall, trying to decide if she should punch an elbow through the glass, when the window swung slowly outward.

Mara froze. The blood pounded in her ears. Had Duke Peyton suspected who she was all along? Had he never gone on the hunt? Had he been waiting for her to break into his study, so he could kill her without anyone knowing?

Nothing stirred in the room. The night had grown silent as though it were also watching and waiting. Perhaps she had managed to un-latch the window after all.

Mara scooted over beneath the window, expectant and uneasy. Cautiously, she placed a hand on the windowsill and pulled herself up until she could peer into the room. Her better judgment told her to give up and retreat because something was clearly not right here. But, if she left now, she might not get another chance. She dragged herself up until she crouched on the windowsill.

The room was dark. It smelled of paper and ink and musty books. Mara dropped lightly to the floor and bent low, careful not to be silhouetted against the window.

The moon had already risen, and the night was not so dark. She scanned the room, trying to let her other senses speak to her. A pe-

The Deadly Jest

culiar smell reached her nose—like a wet dog. The sound of quiet, controlled breathing was barely perceptible.

Mara slipped her fighting sticks from their sheaths and waited. Her mouth went dry. Something shifted in the far corner of the room and then rose.

It was a man.

Mara considered whether she had time to escape out the window and decided she didn't. Every muscle prepared to spring.

"You always have to take the hard way, don't you?"

Jack's voice cut through the darkness.

Mara lunged to her feet as the fury warmed her face.

"You stupid boy," she said in a loud whisper. "I could have killed you."

Jack strode forward until she could see his face. "Not with those things," he said.

It took all the restraint Mara had not to thump him over the head to show him that her fighting sticks were nothing to sniff at.

"How did you get in here?" she demanded.

"I told you I could get you in." The jangle of keys sounded as Jack raised his hand. "I am one of three people the Duke lets into this room."

"You? Why you?" Mara demanded.

Jack shrugged. "I'm more important than you think."

"Well, you might have mentioned you had a key."

Jack grinned. "What? And miss all the fun?"

When she didn't smile in return, he continued.

"You're pretty good, by the way. You didn't make any noise climbing the wall or coming in. I thought you weren't coming until you slipped that piece of metal through the window crack."

"I don't have time for this," Mara said.

She lit a candle and circled the room. A large desk with slots and cubbyholes to hold papers and scrolls filled the center. Shelves with leather-bound books covered one wall, while a fireplace filled most of another. A few trophies of hunts hung on the walls with a couple of swords. It was a room designed for a man.

"What are we looking for?" Jack said.

"I can't tell you," Mara snapped. Arno had warned her not to trust anyone. Jack might be her contact, but he was also close to the Duke.

She didn't know where his loyalties lay.

Jack clicked his tongue in annoyance. "Well, at least tell me if it's a book or a map or piece of paper or what."

"It's a piece of paper signed by the Duke," Mara said.

"Oh, that'll be easy," Jack mocked. "Every letter in here is going to be signed by him."

"Then look for one that mentions the Kingdom of Coll."

Jack stepped to the desk and rummaged through the loose papers in the slots. Mara didn't think the Duke would hide something as important and secret as this letter out in the open like that. He had to have some secret hiding place.

Mara scoured the books, flipping through each one, tapping on the wall behind them. She pulled back the rug, inspected every crack in the floor and walls, combed through every pile of loose papers. They searched for over an hour as Mara became increasingly nervous that the Duke would reappear and find them in his study.

"I don't think it's here," Jack said. "I've gone through every paper on this desk. There's nothing but bills of sale, some maps of the duchy and the kingdom, and a few love notes from Lady Erica." He held one up for Mara to see. "She is apparently a woman of considerable passion."

"I'd rather not know," Mara said.

A cry rang over the quiet castle grounds.

"What was that?" Mara asked.

Jack darted to the window and thrust his head out. The cry came again.

"Someone's at the gate," he said. "Come on." He pulled the window closed and latched it before racing out the door into the Duke's bedroom. Mara followed, hot on his heels.

Jack locked the study door and, together, he and Mara joined a growing crowd of servants, lords, and ladies, all dressed in their nightclothes. Mara yanked her hood up, so she wouldn't be recognized, and scrambled to her room as quickly as she could. She threw on her maid's clothes over the top of her others and then rushed to the great hall to find a crowd gathered around an injured servant who had gone with the Duke on his hunt.

"They took him," the servant said.

"Wait. Start over." The white-haired lord, who had been watching

The Deadly Jest

Mara spoke. "Who attacked you?"

"I don't know, Lord Fendrel," the servant said. "They weren't wearing any colors. We were on our way back with the stag the Duke killed when they came out of the woods with a huge net. They threw it over Duke Peyton and two of his men-at-arms and dragged them away."

"What about Lord Steven and Lord Bryce?"

"They had already separated from us to stay in a tavern that Lord Steven likes."

"And the other guards?"

"Captured."

"I don't believe it," one of the lords said. "Duke Peyton isn't foolish enough to be caught off guard like that."

The servant cowered in front of them. "I only know what I saw."

"Then how did you escape?" Lord Fendrel asked.

"I was at the rear, and no one took any notice of me. I hid until I was the only one free, and I ran to find help."

Lord Fendrel rose and surveyed the crowd.

"I'm the highest ranking lord here," he said. "Does anyone object to my taking the lead?"

The half dozen knights exchanged doubtful glances, but no one challenged him.

"Good. Get the hounds," he said. "And raise the guard. We'll need twenty good men who can ride hard."

Lady Erica bustled in, dressed in a long, pink nightdress with a white cap covering her thick brown hair. Her cheeks flushed.

"What has happened?" she wailed. "Where is my betrothed?"

She swept a dimpled hand to her chest as her gaze fell upon the injured servant. "Is he dead?"

Lord Fendrel raised his eyebrows as the men paused and watched her with interest. Mara glanced at Jack, who was smiling as if he enjoyed her antics.

"Duke Peyton has been kidnapped, My Lady," Lord Fendrel said.

Lady Erica fanned her face her chubby hand. "Oh no," she said. "What will become of me?"

Mara was trying to work out what she meant, when Lady Thea glided into the great hall, followed by her servants.

"What is being done to recover him?" she demanded.

Lord Fendrel bowed to her. "We are organizing a party now, My Lady," he said. "We will depart as soon as may be."

Lady Erica's bosom heaved as she sucked in great gulps of air. "Oh, I feel faint."

She raised a dramatic hand to her forehead and tumbled sideways. Jack tried to catch her, but he disappeared under her bulk as she slid to the ground. Nothing but his twitching feet and arms protruded from beneath her.

Mara jumped to his side and tried to shove Lady Erica off, but she was too heavy. Several men joined her, and together they rolled Lady Erica aside. Her servants darted in to assist her.

Jack sat up and looked around, dazed.

"That was the most horrifying experience of my life," he said. A chorus of snickering sounded behind him.

"Someone get this woman some wine," Lord Fendrel said. He bowed to Lady Thea and strode from the hall followed by the rest of the men.

Mara dragged Jack to his feet, struggling not to smile.

"A bit much for you, was she?" Mara asked.

"I'll meet you in the kitchen," Jack said, smoothing his tunic.

Mara slipped through the door and stood in the shadows by the oven. It was still warm from the day's baking. Jack came in with a scowl on his face.

"If that Lord Doran does anything to the Duke, I'll get even."

"What are you talking about?" Mara asked.

"Well, who else would want to kidnap the Duke?" Then Jack narrowed his eyes. "The Order of the Rook isn't behind this, are they?"

"Of course not," Mara scoffed. "We don't kidnap people without good cause and the assurance that it won't get us involved in wars we don't want to fight."

"Well, I'm going with them to search for him."

Mara grabbed his arm as he spun to hurry away.

"Wait," she said. "I've been thinking. If the letter isn't in the Duke's chambers or in his study, it must be on his person. It may be so sensitive that he has kept it close."

"What are you suggesting?"

"That I track down the kidnappers and rescue the Duke," Mara said, "while you keep searching his rooms."

The Deadly Jest

Jack frowned. "I'm coming with you."

"It's too risky," Mara said with a shake of her head.

"You think the Duke is going to let some maid he doesn't know rescue him?" Jack demanded. "He knows me, and he trusts me. Besides, after what I've seen, you could use some help."

"What's that supposed to mean?"

Jack wiggled his ears at her.

"This isn't some joke," Mara said.

"I'm deadly serious," Jack said. "Duke Peyton is like family to me. He saved me from the streets when I was just a kid. He made sure I was educated and trained in everything he was trained in, and he lets me be his jester. I owe him everything."

Mara considered him. "Then why do you spy on him for the Order?"

"Because I can always use a few extra coins, and he likes to know what you people are up to."

Mara opened her mouth to shout at him and then closed it. "You're a traitor to the Order?" she asked.

Jack shook his head. "I don't belong to the Order," Jack said. "I'm just an informant. And I've never betrayed any secret to him that would hurt the Order or vice versa. But if you ask me to choose between the Order and the Duke, I will choose the Duke every time. What has the Order ever done for me but given me a few coins for a bit of information? The Duke is my family."

Mara couldn't fault his reasoning. The Order of the Rook was her family, and she would do anything to protect it because she had no one else. Arno had found her in a burning castle on Perth and carried her to safety. He had raised her and trained her in all the arts of the assassin and the spy. Despite the arguments against it, he had allowed her to test three years before the usual time, and she was the only woman to have completed the test at all, let alone having done it in record time.

Footsteps slapped the stone floor. Mara grabbed Jack and yanked him into a close embrace. They couldn't be seen talking like this. The door banged open. Jack stiffened in surprise for an instant before he buried his face in her neck and kissed her. Mara resisted the urge to punch him again. He was clearly enjoying this far more than he should. She stared over his shoulder at the doorway as Sarah came to an abrupt halt, her hand still holding the door open. Mara shoved Jack away, and he turned with a big, sloppy smile.

"Oops," he said.

He grabbed Mara's hand and dragged her from the kitchen as an expression of pure hatred slipped across Sarah's face.

When they stepped out into the warm night air, Mara jerked her hand from Jack's grasp.

"You're getting the hang of it," Jack said. "Maybe we should practice some more."

Mara didn't want to think about what had happened, and she wasn't going to admit to anyone that it scared her. She was supposed to be in control of her emotions. But the feel of Jack close to her and the brush of his lips on her neck had ignited a fire in her belly that shouldn't be there. She had a job to do.

"I'll pass," she said. "Can you get us food and water for several days?"

Jack studied her for a moment as if he realized that she had been unbalanced by what they had done. He had the grace not to pursue it.

"You always forget who you're talking to," Jack said.

"Meet me back here then," Mara said, "and bring whatever weapons you've been trained to use." She paused. "Except for the long-sword. You look ridiculous with that thing."

Mara waited in the safety of the shadows as men bustled about packing gear and saddling horses. Jack strolled up to her leading two horses.

"You forgot to mention the horses," Jack said. "So I grabbed one for you." He had slipped on his padded shirt and fighting gloves.

"What took you so long?" she demanded.

Jack passed a hand over his bald head. "I had to shave," he said. "Since I didn't know when I would get the chance again."

"Of course," Mara said, her tone dripping with sarcasm.

"Well, a bald head is cooler during the hot summers," Jack said.

"Don't you wear a cap or something? Your brain's going to fry in this southern heat."

"I don't suppose you noticed my beautiful tan," Jack said.

The Deadly Jest

Mara snorted and glanced at the short sword and dagger Jack had strapped to his waist.

"Is that your preferred weapon?" she asked, pointing to the sword.

"Pretty much," Jack said. "I like a good bow, but I wasn't sure how much crawling around in the woods we're going to have to do."

Mara grabbed the reins of one of the horses, and they headed toward the gate.

"What about you?" Jack said, glancing at the sticks on her back. "Do you only use the fighting sticks?"

"No. I've been trained to use any weapon, but I prefer a spear or a glaive," she said. "Still, it's tough to climb walls and sneak into tight places with a six-foot pole strapped to you. Besides, I don't always want to kill or leave blood, so the fighting sticks are better."

"Why are you an assassin if you don't like to kill?" Jack questioned.

Mara frowned. "I'm only an assassin when I have to be."

"Seems like you picked the wrong profession."

Mara stared at him as the frustrated anger welled up inside her. Why did Jack have to be so perceptive? She had tried to hide her abhorrence of killing from everyone. She enjoyed the challenge of combat and the thrill of danger. What disturbed her was the way the life left the eyes as people died. The way an animated human body became nothing more than an empty shell. She shivered.

"It's the only option I ever had," Mara said.

They mounted and fell in with the knot of men that rode out through the gate. No one seemed to notice Mara in all the confusion. Once they passed into the city, she fell back so she wouldn't attract attention. The men rode hard for twenty minutes but slowed once they reached the forest.

The woods closed around them as they entered the foothills beyond the city of Kirn. The moon cast the floor of the forest in a patchwork of shifting shadows. Mara sat astride her horse. She wore her mottled cloak and dark clothes. The reassuring presence of her fighting sticks and knives strapped to her body gave her a sense of safety she hadn't felt since donning the maid's dress.

They hadn't traveled more than a mile under the canopy of trees when the men in front stopped. A narrow path broke off from the main road and crossed over a bridge that allowed only two horses to cross at a time. The men dismounted, and Mara followed their example before slipping into the trees and ghosting toward the bridge. She wanted to see and hear what was going on without attracting attention. Jack followed her.

A dozen men-at-arms stood with their backs to the trees. Four of them slumped against the ropes that bound them, and Mara guessed that they had been injured. The servant's voice rang out in the quiet of the night.

"They went that way," he said, gesturing toward the south.

"How many were there?" someone asked.

"I don't know. Forty or fifty."

"Cut these men loose," Lord Fendrel said, "and treat their injuries. We'll send them back in the wagon. It should be here in an hour or so."

Some men sprang into the woods in the direction the servant pointed, but Lord Fendrel yelled for them to stop.

"Let the tracker check it out first," he said. "You'll trample the trail." He gestured to the men behind him. "Bring those hounds up."

"Look at this," someone shouted and held up a piece of cloth. "It was snagged on this bush."

Mara crept closer to have a better look as someone bent in with a torch to examine it.

"It's yellow," he said. "That's the Baron of Longmire's colors."

"Would he really stoop this low because of a dispute over a spring and a few cattle?" one of the men asked.

"Looks like it," Lord Fendrel said. "But let's follow the trail to see which way they went."

A tall, thin man stepped in front of the others with a torch in his hand and bent to examine the trail.

Jack loomed over Mara's shoulder to whisper in her ear.

"Longmire wouldn't do that," he said.

"What?"

"The Baron of Longmire didn't need to capture Duke Peyton," he said. "They had already agreed on a solution. The Duke told me about it yesterday."

"Then who would take him?"

Jack shrugged.

"You think they left a false trail to implicate the Baron of Longmire?" Mara asked.

The Deadly Jest

Jack pursed his lips and made a funny face.

"Stop that and answer the question." Mara nudged him with her elbow.

"Looks like it," he said.

"I'll be back," Mara said. "You stay with them and see what they find."

Jack tried to protest, but Mara ignored him. She stole back to where she had left her horse and ducked into the undergrowth to circle around in the opposite direction. If someone had been trying to mislead any pursuers, there might be another trail out there that would indicate where they were going.

The forest smelled fresh and alive with the rich scent of earth and the occasional sweet aroma of flowers. Nairn didn't have many trees and no real forests, but Mara had always loved the woods. She took a deep breath, savoring the smell. The creek wiggled through the wood, and she followed it since it went in the general direction she wanted to go. It was also the most likely spot to find evidence in the dark if someone had passed.

She hadn't gone more than a hundred yards, when a ray of moonlight illuminated a deep bootprint in the mud of the bank. Mara bent and touched the mud with her finger. It was firm. Only a heavy man could have made such a deep print—or a man carrying a heavy load. Mara fell to her knees, wishing she had a torch to help her see.

On careful inspection, she found two more sets of bootprints, but no hoofprints. These men were on foot, carrying something heavy, and they were heading east, not southwest toward Longmire. She followed the trail, careful not to step on it. It was hard enough following a trail in the dark. She didn't need to pollute it by being careless.

Foot by foot, she made her way painstakingly through the shadowed wood. When she lost the trail, she guessed the direction they were traveling and crept ahead until she found it again. Another hundred yards brought her to a tiny clearing where the grass had been trampled by the hooves of many horses. The trail leading from there was broad, and it still headed east.

Mara circled the clearing to be sure she didn't miss another trail before she crept back to the bridge and her horse. Jack's horse was gone. The men-at-arms had all been cut loose and were eating and drinking. Mara paused. How was she going to get around them unseen to tell Jack that she had found the trail?

The sound of pounding hooves brought everyone's head up as a rider broke from the trees. It was Jack.

"They found the other two guards," he said to the few men Lord Fendrel had left behind. "But the Duke is gone. Lord Fendrel says that he's taking the rest of the men and the dogs in pursuit."

Jack rode up to where Mara crouched in the shadows.

"Well?" he asked.

"I found the trail," Mara said.

"Let's go then."

Mara climbed into the saddle and reined her horse. She ducked into the trees as she rode toward the clearing. She didn't pause there because she had already checked it. The broad trail was easy to see, so she kicked her horse to follow it.

"They're heading east," she said. "Does the Duke have any enemies in the east?"

"The Duke doesn't have many enemies yet," Jack said. "He just became a duke six months ago when his father died. But that Lord Doran was from the Barony of Cassel. It's east of here."

"If he had wanted to kill him," Mara observed, "I think he would have done it outright. Do you think they want to hold him for a ransom?"

"I don't think the King would allow it," Jack said. "I mean, the barons are often at each other's throats and do some raiding, but kidnapping a duke who is related to the King would be a big deal. You'd have to be crazy—or desperate."

Mara sighed. "Well, there's only one way to find out. I hope you can sleep in the saddle," she said.

"I can sleep anywhere," Jack said and winked at her.

Mara stood on the green hillside holding her horse's reins. They had followed the trail for four days through the foothills, across the rolling plain to the Wolf River. To avoid detection, they had split the watch during the night, camped without fire, and avoided people.

The kidnappers might have had spies among the local populace or scouts watching their back trail. Avoiding populated areas hadn't

The Deadly Jest

been too difficult. The captors had bypassed all towns and villages until they came to where the north and east roads met. The trail had gone cold as the kidnappers took to the east road. It was impossible to distinguish the riders she was following from the dozens of hoofprints and wagon tracks that marred the road.

Mara climbed to the nearest hill, trying to decide her next move. Jack had gone to a nearby village to see if anyone had seen the riders. This mission was already taking longer than expected. By now, she should have been heading back to Royan.

It had occurred to her that someone had kidnapped the Duke to get the same letter she was after, which left her with a sick feeling in her gut. If the Duke did have the letter on him, they would have taken it by now. But that didn't explain why they hadn't let him go or killed him. The Hallstat might be involved in more than one conspiracy, or perhaps agents from Coll had somehow received word of the planned invasion and kidnapped the Duke to get the details.

Mara spun at the sound of someone climbing the hill. Jack rode his horse up the gentle slope. For a moment, Mara wondered what he would look like with hair. It was a crazy thought that made her smile.

"What?" Jack said. He had seen her trying to hide her smile behind a raised hand.

"I was trying to imagine you with hair," she said. "Somehow I couldn't."

Jack dismounted. "That's because a bald head is a beautiful thing," he said and passed a hand over his head. "Women always prefer bald-headed men."

"Do they?" Mara asked.

"Oh yeah," Jack said. "Bald men are smarter. They make better lovers and fighters."

"You do remember that you just shave your head, right?" Mara said. "I mean, you aren't really bald."

"It's all in the perception." Jack raised his eyebrows at her.

Mara shook her head and gazed out over the rolling countryside. "Find anything?" she asked.

"Of course," Jack said. "No one can resist my charms."

"Sure," Mara said. "So what did you find?"

"They came this way," Jack said. "I found one old man who said

105

he heard they had gone to Waterstone Manor."

"Where's that?"

"It's less than a day's ride from here."

The humor in his voice made Mara peer at him. He had a knowing grin on his face.

"So why are you smiling?" Mara pulled her horse closer to Jack.

"You'll never guess."

Mara sighed. "I don't have to guess because you're going to tell me."

Jack wiggled his ears. "Waterstone Manor is the summer residence of the Earl of Mayen," he said as if this should mean something to her.

"So?"

"So, Lady Alicia is his daughter."

"The thin one?" Mara gasped. "You're joking."

"Even *I* couldn't have come up with a joke like this," Jack said and chuckled.

"I thought you said they were just friends." Mara couldn't believe it. Something more than a mere kidnapping was going on here.

"Down," Jack snapped and fell to his belly in the grass.

Mara sneered at him. "Stop trying to scare me."

Jack waved at her to get down. "I'm not trying to scare you. Get down, or they'll see you."

Mara whipped around to gaze out over the road as a long line of horsemen with a lady dressed in a fine dress riding sidesaddle. Mara dropped to her belly on the hillside. The rich smell of disturbed earth and crushed grass filled her nostrils. Jack belly-crawled over to her.

"That's Lady Alicia," he said.

Mara looked at him. "How could she be here already unless…"

"Unless she knew the Duke would be captured and taken to Waterstone Manor?" Jack finished for her. "She must have left earlier that day. I don't remember seeing her at dinner. Do you?"

"No," Mara said. "And she didn't come down when we received word that the Duke had been kidnapped."

"That's because she had already left," Jack said.

"Do you think she wants to hold him for ransom?" Mara asked.

Jack grinned again. "Of a sort," he said. "I used to think there was something between them when they were younger, but the Duke's father signed a contract with the Duke of Einbeck that Peyton could only marry Lady Erica."

"Wait," Mara said. "You mean that Lady Alicia kidnapped Duke Peyton to force him to marry her?"

"Yep." Jack winked at her. "It's kind of romantic, isn't it?"

"It's sick," Mara said, wrinkling her nose.

"Maybe," Jack said, "but if we don't get him out and she can get him to bed her, he'll be duty-bound to marry her."

"That's really sick," Mara said. "He wouldn't fall for something like that, would he?"

Jack shrugged. "She *is* pretty."

"And that's all a man cares about?" Mara snapped.

Jack pursed his lips. "No, but it helps."

Mara watched the riders as their horses cantered around a low hill and disappeared into a thin woodland. What if she had been Lady Alicia? Would she have been willing to force a man to marry her? Could a woman who coerced a man into marriage ever know if he loved her? Did it matter? Maybe marriage among nobles was only about political and economic alliances. Mara wondered what her parents had felt for each other. Had they been in love? Had they loved her?

Mara shook herself. She didn't have time for useless brooding.

"Look," she said, "I don't care who he marries. I just need that letter."

"Well, I do care," Jack said. "We can't let Duke Peyton get forced into a disagreeable marriage because of some old custom."

"You Hallstat are strange," Mara said. "Whoever heard of such an idea?"

Mara led her horse down the hill so she could mount without being silhouetted against the skyline.

"Well, let's get him out tonight," she said. "Lead the way to Waterstone Manor."

The sun drooped low on the western horizon before they reached the manor. It was nestled in a beautiful valley with a wide, shallow creek winding through it. Fields and pastures surrounded the buildings with golden grain waving in the breeze and shaggy cattle roaming the hillsides. A broad lawn spread out in front of the manor with a wide lane leading up to the walls.

The hulking manor was more of a small castle with a full curtain wall and a tower protecting the gate. Beyond the walls stood the square, palatial structure with a single high tower jutting up from one corner. A brown and orange banner waved above the tower. They didn't have much time to plan, so they lay on their bellies on a nearby hill, trying to work out what to do.

"I know where the entrance to the sewer is," Jack said.

Mara studied him. "Why would you know that?" she asked.

"When you're a boy with nothing to do, you find things."

Mara waved a hand at him. "Forget it," she said. "I don't want to know. But I'm not climbing in through a sewer."

"Not even for the Order?" Jack said with a wink.

Mara chose to ignore him. "First, we have to find out where he is," she said.

"That's easy," Jack said. "Everyone here knows me."

"But they won't expect you to show up now."

"Yes, they will," Jack said. "The Duke knows I'm not as stupid as the rest of them."

"All right," Mara surrendered. "You go in, find out where he is, and then we'll plan."

Jack somersaulted down the hill to his horse. Mara tried to figure out how he did that without getting himself tangled in his sword. A part of her wished she could be so carefree.

"I'll just tell them I followed Lady Alicia after I saw her leave," he said as he vaulted into the saddle. Then he galloped over the hill toward the manor.

He didn't return until the sun was well gone and the crickets and night owls had started singing. A canopy of stars swung overhead. Mara's belly ached as she nibbled on a crust of hard bread. What she wouldn't give for the delicious pastries for which Nairn was justly famous. Some were filled with meat and onions while others were stuffed with ripe berries and slathered in honey. The thought of those pastries made her stomach rumble.

Jack moseyed up the hill toward her as if he didn't have a care in the world—as if they weren't pressed for time. He patted his belly and flopped down beside her.

"Well?" she asked.

"Well, that was one delicious pie," he said.

Mara gave him an indignant glance. "You sat down there and ate a pie?" she demanded.

"They offered," Jack said. "It would have been rude to say no." He held out a roll and wedge of cheese he had wrapped in a cloth. "I got this for you," he said.

Mara lifted it from his hand and grimaced. "Thanks. That was real thoughtful of you." She tore off a bite, savoring the soft, buttery flavor.

"I know," he said.

Mara rolled her eyes. "What did you find out?"

"He's in his usual room getting ready for dinner," Jack said.

"His usual room?" Mara asked.

"The families visit each other regularly," Jack said. "That's how everyone here knows me."

"Right. Do you know a way in?"

Jack rubbed his chin in thought. "Do you want to go in the hard way or the easy way?"

"The fast way," Mara said. "The way we are least likely to be seen."

Jack grinned. "I spread the word among the guards and the staff that I was going to play a trick on the Duke," he said. "To surprise him. They won't give us any trouble."

"Is this something you do regularly?"

Jack spread his hands. "That's what he pays me for."

Mara shook her head. "You're insane. You know that?"

She finished the roll and started on the cheese. It was tangy, the way she liked it.

"Just creative," he said.

"So what's your plan?" Mara asked between bites.

"How good are you at climbing ropes?" Jack asked.

"Good," Mara said.

"I never met a lady who climbed ropes," Jack said.

"I'm a spy," she shrugged.

"Right. Then let's go," Jack said. "We only have an hour."

Jack and Mara slipped into the castle through an obscure door at the back and made their way around to the side where Jack looked up and pointed.

"That's his room up there," he said.

Mara glanced up to find a balcony, where a pair of tall windows allowed access to the room. A pale, yellow light flickered inside the glass.

"Are you sure?"

"When are you going to start trusting me?" Jack demanded.

"I'm not," Mara said, smiling sweetly at him.

He pulled out a grappling hook, secured a rope to it, and swung the rope back and forth as he prepared to throw it. Mara grabbed his arm.

"He'll hear you," she said. "Give me that."

She snatched the rope from his hand, draped the grappling hook over her shoulder, and climbed. The manor was even easier to climb than the Duke's castle had been, and she was on the balcony in a matter of minutes. After attaching the grappling hook to the sturdiest beam, she motioned for Jack to climb. He came up hand-over-hand as if he weighed nothing at all. The two of them crouched on the balcony and peered in.

Mara sucked in her breath and averted her gaze. Jack shook with suppressed laughter.

"He's bathing," Mara mouthed.

The Duke sat half-submerged in a copper tub with his back to them. Several pitchers of water stood on a side table with a towel and a change of clothes.

"That he is," Jack said. "He's a fine looking specimen of manhood, don't you think?"

"I'm not going in there with him naked," Mara whispered. The warm blush rose in her cheeks. "You go in and get him. I'll wait here."

Jack pursed his lips. "That's probably best," he said. "I'm not sure how he'd react to a cute young woman strolling in while he's bathing to tell him she has come to rescue him after he's already been kidnapped by another woman."

"Just hurry up," Mara said. "And make him dress."

She struggled to understand the nature of Jack's relationship with

The Deadly Jest

the Duke. Mara had never known a noble who would tolerate the things Jack got up to. And here they were invading his privacy in a most intimate way. The Duke could have them thrown into chains or executed on the spot. Jack was taking a serious risk.

Duke Peyton faced away from them. His arms stretched out over the edge of the copper tub and his head lay back as if he were enjoying a much needed rest.

Jack pushed on the window. It didn't open, so Mara slipped in her thin piece of metal and lifted the latch. Jack crept in on cat's feet, picked up a pitcher of water from a table, and dumped it over the Duke's head.

The Duke burst from the water with a tremendous splash, and Mara whipped around to avoid seeing him naked, but she could hear him yell.

"Muck, you scoundrel!" he shouted. "I can't even get away from you when I'm kidnapped. I'll have you horsewhipped for this one."

"Actually," Jack said. "I came to tell you that you're in danger. You need to leave."

Mara chanced a glance. Duke Peyton had already slipped into a tunic that fell almost to his knees. The tunic clung to his wet body. Mara looked away as he pulled on a pair of trousers.

"What are you talking about?" Duke Peyton asked.

Jack's voice became serious, which was unusual.

"We know what Lady Alicia is up to," Jack said. "And you have another problem. Lord Fendrel is leading a group of armed men to the Baron of Longmire's lands in search of you."

"What? Why?"

Mara peeked again. The Duke cinched a belt tight over his tunic.

"They found a piece of cloth from a Longmire tunic," Jack said. "One of Lord Fendrel's men found it."

"That pompous windbag," Duke Peyton said. "I never could see why Father liked him."

"So," Jack insisted, "we have to get you out of here before it's too late and before Lord Fendrel starts a war with Longmire."

"Wait," the Duke said. "Who is we?"

Jack's gaze strayed to the window where Mara crouched. She slipped in and lowered her hood.

"I know you," Duke Peyton said.

"I'm Mara from the Order of the Rook," she said.

The Duke sighed and raised his gaze to the ceiling as if to ask for divine assistance. "What do you people want?" he asked.

"We're here to rescue you, obviously," she said.

Duke Peyton fell into a chair. "I don't want to be rescued," he said.

"Oh, don't tell us that." Jack slapped his legs in disbelief. "Not after five days of searching for you."

Mara stared at the Duke, trying to work out why he wouldn't want them to rescue him. The entire thing was so farcical, she almost laughed. A powerful man carried off and forced to wed a woman against his will? Nowhere else in the world would such a thing be tolerated, even if the woman had an army at her disposal.

"I already married her," Duke Peyton said.

"What?" Mara exclaimed. She threw up her hands in disbelief. Was the Duke crazy?

Jack guffawed.

"You married a woman who kidnapped you?" Mara asked, still unable to accept that he was telling them the truth.

"Well, consider the alternative," Duke Peyton said. "Did you meet Lady Erica?"

"You know, he has a point," Jack said. Mara knew he was thinking of Lady Erica's antics the night the Duke went missing.

"My father arranged for me to marry that loud-mouthed simpleton," the Duke said, "because her father has connections at court. This was the only way out. If I refused, she could bring a suit against me. But if I was kidnapped and forced into it, the law says she can't come after me for breach of contract."

"Wait," Jack said in disbelief. "You were in on it?"

The Duke shrugged and avoided Jack's gaze.

"Desperate times call for desperate measures," he said. A smile crept over his face.

"That's the most ridiculous law I ever heard," Mara said. "It basically lets anyone kidnap and rape someone else to force them to marry them."

The Duke nodded. "That's about right."

Mara shook her head. "And we wasted five days trying to rescue you."

"That's hardly my fault," Duke Peyton said. "Now, if you don't mind, I think I will join my wife for a quiet dinner."

"You can't," Mara exclaimed.

"What?" Duke Peyton said.

Even Jack blinked at her in surprise.

Mara blushed. "I mean, please, Your Grace. Just give me that wretched document you drew up with King Tristan."

Duke Peyton stared at her with his mouth open. "How do you know about that?"

"I'm a spy," Mara said. "And the Order needs to see that document."

"I don't have it," Duke Peyton said as if Mara were as dumb as a post. "I was kidnapped, you know."

Mara's heart sank. "Then where is it?" she asked.

Duke Peyton scowled. "Go home."

Mara wanted to grab the Duke's collar and make him speak, but she thought better of it and sighed.

"Please, Your Grace," she said. "You know the Order won't let anyone know you've shown it to me."

Duke Peyton gawked at her like she had lost her mind. "To give you that letter would be an act of treason."

"Don't you think you owe us something?" Mara asked.

"For what? Being fool enough to chase me halfway across the kingdom? The mere fact that I don't arrest you and execute you for even knowing about this letter is my reward for your service. Now leave me alone, or I'll call the guard."

"Wait a minute," Jack said. "You mean you never had it?"

Duke Peyton frowned. "I had it, but it was stolen the day before I was kidnapped. I didn't just go hunting, I was looking for the knave who pilfered it."

Mara dropped onto the step that led to the balcony. She couldn't believe this. Everything had gone wrong from the beginning.

"Why would someone steal the letter and then go hide in the woods?" Jack said.

The Duke passed his hands over his face.

"A man dressed as a peasant came to the castle seeking alms. I let him stay the night, and the next morning the letter and the peasant were both gone. My men tracked him into the hills."

"Did you find him?" Jack questioned.

"Yes."

"And?" Jack waved his hand for the Duke to continue.

"And he didn't have it and was too simple to have stolen it."

"So you have no idea where it is?"

"No. I have men looking for it, but if I don't recover it, the King will not take it kindly."

Mara raised her head. "Why were you surprised about Longmire?" she asked. "Isn't that what you planned? Didn't you leave the cloth to mislead anyone who tried to follow you?"

"We didn't leave any cloth," the Duke said.

Mara glanced at Jack. "Someone planted it."

"Who?"

"The white-haired man," Mara said. "What's his name?"

"Lord Fendrel." The Duke stared at her and then narrowed his eyes.

"Your Grace?" she said.

"I *thought* he was up to something," Duke Peyton said, "when he appeared out of nowhere. I saw him lurking about the west wing. I thought he had been fiddling with the maids again, but..."

Mara dropped her head into her hands. She had been so stupid. Lord Fendrel had stolen the letter while Jack fought his duel. If she had been thinking straight, she could have beaten him to it. If she hadn't been thinking of Jack.

She stood. "I'll be on my way," she said.

"Hang on," Jack said. "We just got here."

"Lord Fendrel is trying to start a border war between Kirn and Longmire," she said. "And he has that letter. You can sit around and eat pie, but I have a job to do." She stepped out the window.

"Wait," Jack said.

"If you're right," Duke Peyton said, "then Lord Fendrel is guilty of treason." He pondered for a moment. "All right," he said. "If you can recover the letter, I'll let you make a copy of it. But I need you to bring the real one to me."

Mara faced him. "Thank you, Your Grace," she said.

"In return for your service," Duke Peyton said, "I will turn a blind eye to the fact that you've been spying in my castle and trying to undermine Morcia's foreign policy."

Mara knew the Order would protect her from anything the Duke might try, but it would be wise to cultivate a relationship with the Duke. She bowed to him.

"Thank you again," she said before leaping lightly over the railing and grabbing the rope.

"Wait a minute," the Duke said. He stepped to a writing table and scratched a few lines on a piece of paper. Then he slipped his ring from his finger, melted some sealing wax on the letter and pushed his ring into it. He handed the letter to Jack.

"Take this to my steward, Lord Dain," he said. "It tells him to arrest Lord Fendrel and send a missive with my seal to the Baron of Longmire to inform him that these men acted without my knowledge or my orders and that our agreement still stands if he will accept it."

"Yes, My Lord," Jack said.

Mara let herself down the rope. When she looked up, Jack and the Duke were peering down at her.

"You might want to go with her," the Duke said. "And pick up some supplies from the kitchen on your way." He laid a hand on Jack's shoulder. "I know I can trust you, Muck, even though you collect money from the Order from time to time."

Jack shrugged.

Duke Peyton rubbed a hand over Jack's bald head. "And don't get killed in the process. I rather like your dog tricks."

Jack leapt over the railing and lowered himself down. He waved at the Duke and followed Mara out of the courtyard.

The silver-blue flash of lightening ripped through the sky as Mara and Jack huddled under a rock overhang on the southern flank of the Kirn Mountains. The sky had faded from the gray of evening to the black of night in a matter of minutes as the clouds rolled in. Rain pounded the earth around them turning the creek below into a muddy, frothing torrent. They hadn't had time to collect firewood before the storm burst upon them. Luck had led them to this overhang before they were soaked.

Mara clutched her thin cloak tight and shivered. It never ceased to surprise her how a country that was almost always hot could become so chill from a simple rain shower.

Jack sat with his knees drawn up, watching flashes of light lance across the landscape. Their horses huddled close together with their heads bent against the onslaught. There had been no room for them in the overhang. Jack shifted.

"So, what's it like being an assassin?" he asked.

Mara glanced at him.

"I mean how did you become one? You're kind of young."

She shrugged before she realized he couldn't see it.

"I'm not supposed to talk about it," she said.

"We're friends," Jack said. "And you should know by now that you can trust me."

"I was raised by them," Mara said. "Arno pulled me from a burning castle when I was a baby and made sure I was trained."

"So, do you have to kill a lot of people?"

Mara stared out into the darkness. "A few," she said. "It's mostly espionage."

"How many members of the Order are there?"

"I don't know. Only the masters know that."

"Masters?"

"There are thirteen of them. They oversee everything. The six Masters of Assassins do all the training. The six Masters of the Rook manage all of our operations on the islands and mainlands. The Grand Master is the oldest and most experienced. He is the head of the High Council of Thirteen. "

Jack grunted. "So why did they send you here?"

"I finished my apprenticeship, but before I can become a full Journeyman Assassin, I have to complete one mission on my own. Until then, I'm just a candidate."

Jack remained silent for a while. "Do you want to be a full member?" he asked.

Mara stared at his dark shape huddled against the stones beside her.

"Why wouldn't I?"

"It's just that I heard the Order can be evil," he said. "They can kill innocent people and destabilize whole kingdoms just so they can get rich."

"That's not true..." Mara began. Then stopped. It was true. Arno had said as much. He had told her that sometimes the masters made mistakes. That sometimes they did more harm than good.

"It's a job," she said. "I'd rather do this than wait on tables and clean chamber pots. Besides, they taught me how to survive."

The wind shifted and sent rain spraying under the overhang. Jack scooted out of the way so that he was sitting against Mara. She couldn't move over. There was no more room.

"But if you have to travel around on these missions," Jack continued, "do you ever get to settle down anywhere?"

Mara hadn't thought about it. The Order was her family. The Isle of Nairn was her home. Did she want to settle anywhere else?

"What about you?" she asked. "Are you going to be a jester for the rest of your life?" Mara needed to shift the focus of the discussion from herself.

"What else can I do?" Jack said. "I'm nobody. No one even knows who my parents were."

"Do you remember her?" Mara asked in a quiet voice.

"Who?" Jack questioned.

"Your mother."

"Oh, yeah. I mean a little bit. She was tall and slender with long dark hair. I remember that she smelled like apples."

Mara looked at him. "Apples? Really?"

"That's what I remember."

Mara bowed her head. "I don't remember anything. Well, sometimes, I think I can remember someone singing to me."

She shivered and pulled her cloak tighter. Her clothes were so damp that it did little good.

Jack draped an arm around her shoulders and pulled her close. "You're cold," he said.

Mara stiffened and then leaned into him. She was cold and tired.

"Can you believe Duke Peyton married Lady Alicia after she kidnapped him?" Mara asked.

"Of course," Jack said. "But I would only marry for love."

"Sarah likes you," Mara said.

"What?"

"Trust me," Mara said. "I'm a spy."

Jack seemed to think on that for a few moments before he spoke again.

"How does that make you feel?"

"Sarah? She can like whoever she wants."

"You're avoiding my question."

Mara had spent her entire life training and working to become a full member of the Order. She hadn't had time to think about anything else. There hadn't been any other female assassins on Nairn.

"I belong to the Order," Mara said, because her insides were doing funny things, creating strange emotions she had never felt.

Jack lapsed into silence.

Mara stared out at the pounding rain, sure that she had injured him but uncertain what to do about it.

"I could use a hot meal and a warm bed," Jack said as they rode into the city of Kirn. "Eight days in the saddle gets a man mighty sore."

Evening had already fallen. Long shadows cast by the moon that dangled overhead filled the streets. The smell of cooking food wafted through the air to compete with the constant stink of the streets. A few dogs nosed amid the rubbish, and ragtag children struggled for the same scraps.

This kind of thing always left Mara with a feeling of disgust. How could any society condemn children to live in the streets like this and do nothing to help them? On Nairn, the Order made sure everyone had an income and no one went hungry. The Order had a saying: "Hunger and want are the play things of rebellion."

One little ruffian stopped to stare at them and then tore off through the streets.

"I don't think he likes the look of you," Mara said to Jack.

"I usually cause people to swoon—just ask Lady Erica," Jack said with a laugh as they neared the market area and entered the wide street that led to the castle gates. The street was deserted, and the guard fires were not burning on the castle walls. The boy slipped into a side street.

"Something's not right," Mara said.

Jack drew the sword he wore at his hip. Neither of them wore armor, though Jack still had his padded shirt. They had been interested in speed when tracking the Duke. Mara dropped the reins and drew one of her fighting sticks. Then she slipped a throwing knife from

The Deadly Jest

the sheath on her arm. A horse whinnied, and Jack's horse answered.

Five horsemen in mail armor burst from the side street to their left where the boy had disappeared. Lord Doran rode at their head, his long hair flowing behind him. He didn't have a helmet—probably because Jack had ruined his.

Jack whirled to face them. "It's the great nostrilled knave!" he yelled. Their swords clashed.

Mara cocked back her arm as another rider came up on the other side of Jack. She threw. Her blade tumbled through the air to bury itself in the man's eye. He went limp and slipped from his saddle to tumble onto the road.

Jack vaulted from his saddle and hit the ground running. Lord Doran followed with one of his men. The other two came after Mara.

She kicked her horse into a side street and galloped toward the castle. She would have given anything for a spear or a glaive at this moment. But all she had were a few knives and her fighting sticks. She rounded a corner and jumped from the horse's back. The horse slowed, but she gave it a slap to keep it running. Then she climbed toward the flat roof of a shop.

The riders galloped around the corner. Mara swung her fighting stick straight into the face of the first rider. The shock of the blow made her hand go numb.

Her stick struck below the noseguard on his helmet, slamming into his chin with a loud crack before it deflected into his throat. He gave a strangled cry and crumpled sideways, struggling to stay astride the horse.

The second rider pulled his horse to a halt, but Mara was already on the roof and running.

She had to find Jack. He was alone, without armor, facing two men. She circled back to the street he had taken. Two horses lay on the cobblestones. One of them still struggled feebly as its life's blood spilled over the street. But there was no sign of Jack.

The clash of steel echoed through the streets. The roofs slanted upward abruptly, causing Mara to drop to the ground. Jack's voice rang through the streets, followed by the crash of steel.

"Your bulbous beak seems to be in your way," he called.

Mara sprinted around a corner into a courtyard with a fountain.

Jack had positioned himself between a cart and the fountain so that Lord Doran and his man-at-arms could only come at him one at a time.

Blood bathed one side of Jack's face.

Mara raced to his aid, pulling out her fighting sticks. The sticks were specially built with steel strips to allow her to use them against bladed weapons. Lord Doran pressed Jack hard from the front.

The man-at-arms scrambled around the wagon to come up behind Jack. He reached the back of the wagon and raised his arm for a blow when Mara's first strike cracked against the wrist of the hand that held his sword.

The second struck his collarbone. The third slammed into his throat. The man gurgled something and fell heavily against the wagon.

Jack was visibly tiring and had quit shouting his usual insults. Lord Doran bore a wicked grin.

"Your Duke is finished," Lord Doran said. "And so are you."

Mara jumped up on the lip of the fountain and leapt toward Lord Doran. He tried to deflect her sticks, but they whirled so fast that he only managed to stop one strike.

The other slammed into the side of his head as Jack plunged his blade into Lord Doran's throat. Lord Doran's eyes opened wide. He understood that he was about to die.

Mara looked away. She had never liked seeing the light leave people's eyes.

The clatter of horse hooves against stone echoed in the small courtyard, and Mara spun to find the last rider bearing down upon them. When he saw that Lord Doran had fallen, he reined the horse around and raced toward the castle.

Jack smiled at Mara through the blood that drenched his face.

"Well, that was a nice welcome home," he said.

"Are you all right?" Mara asked.

Jack nodded. "It's not too bad. But I think we should get to the castle. Something is very wrong."

Mara tore a strip of cloth from Jack's tunic and tied it around his head.

"Scars are supposed to be attractive on men," she said.

"I knew you liked me," Jack said.

The Deadly Jest

Mara grinned back at him in spite of herself. Jack was incorrigible.

He sheathed his sword, and they sprinted toward the castle. When they reached the edge of the market, Mara pulled him into an empty stall to study the situation.

Jack grinned at her. "What? You want to practice being betrothed some more?" he asked.

It took Mara several moments to understand what he meant. "What?" she said.

"I hardly think this is the time or place," Jack said.

"Be serious," Mara said.

"Okay. You want to climb in again?" Jack asked.

"No," she said. "Just checking things out before we go blundering in."

Mara struggled with indecision. Arno had instructed her to get out if the mission went bad. Well, the mission had gone from bad to worse. She didn't know where the letter was—or if it was even still at the castle.

Apparently, a coup was taking place against the Duke. No guards patrolled the walls, no watch fires had been lit. She didn't have any authorization to get involved in the internal politics of Morcia. Maybe she should cut her losses and get out before she involved the Order in things it wanted to avoid.

She glanced at Jack. He looked comical with the bandage tied around his head. His face was tight with worry. His friends lived in the castle. He was going in to help them no matter what she did. She may not have a mother or a real family, but she did have friends.

Arno trusted her. Jack trusted her, and he would need her help to survive the night. Duke Peyton was relying on her to recover the letter and save him from the political scandal its loss might cause. In so doing, she might be able to turn him and Lady Alicia into valuable allies. She couldn't turn her back on all of that.

"We may as well enter through the gate this time," Mara said.

Jack rose and faced her. "You know you don't have to go in there to help me," he said. "I want you to know, in case anything happens, that I really do care for you. Thanks for putting up with me." He reached out and squeezed her hand.

Mara was surprised by his declaration—but more surprised at the warmth that spread in her chest and the tightness in her throat.

J.W. Elliot

"That's what friends do," she said.

Jack nodded. "I think we need to find Lord Dain and Lady Thea," he said. "We need to make sure they're safe."

They kept to the shadows as much as possible while working their way toward the residential part of the castle. Candles burned in some of the windows, but the grounds were strangely quiet. The barracks and stables were empty. All the men-at-arms had ridden away. They encountered a few guards, but Jack avoided them.

He led Mara into the castle through the servants' entrance and into the servants' hallways. They worked their way up through the deserted passages to the west wing where Duke Peyton's family lived, until they could slip out into the main corridor. They found Lady Thea's room, and Jack gave a quiet knock. No one answered, so he lifted the latch and pushed the door ajar. Mara peered over his head. Perfumed air swept over them, and Mara considered how badly she must smell after ten days without a bath.

Lady Thea sat board-straight on a padded chair with her hands folded in her lap. Her maids stood beside her. Two men, dressed in the yellow colors of the Baron of Longmire, watched over them. They each wore mail shirts and steel helmets. They both wore swords and long knives. One of them brandished a spear.

"What is it?" the guard without the spear demanded.

Jack stepped into the room. A gasp arose from the women as they recognized him. The guards apparently didn't know him. Mara checked the hallway and followed Jack in before closing the door behind her.

"Who are you?" Jack demanded. "And why are you here?"

The guard frowned and stepped toward Jack, placing a hand on the pommel of his sword.

"Look, little man," the guard said. "You should just leave now."

Jack jammed his hands on his hips. "You're not from Longmire," he said. "You have a southern accent. You're from Eliff, aren't you?" Jack imitated the accent.

The guards glanced at one another. Lady Thea rose and backed away from the guards as she shooed her maids behind her. Something metallic flashed in her hand before she slipped it beneath the sleeve of her dress.

Mara pulled her fighting sticks from their sheaths as Jack drew his

The Deadly Jest

sword. She stepped up beside Jack.

"You really should get out," the guard said, "before you get hurt."

"I've already been hurt," Jack said. "But that didn't stop me."

Jack faked a strike to the soldier's face with his sword.

As the man raised his sword to deflect the blow, Jack dove to the floor, rolled, and swept his sword into the back of the man's leg in a crippling strike to the hamstring.

At the same instant, the guard with the spear lunged at Mara.

She deflected the powerful thrust with her sticks but not before it cut a shallow gash in her side.

She rolled her body around the shaft, trapped it under her arm and struck the man's helmet.

A loud clang sounded.

The man jerked on the spear.

Mara struck him on the side of the neck.

He stumbled.

She brought the stick down on his collarbone with a loud crack.

Mara jerked the spear from his grasp and tossed it across the room as he curled up to protect his broken bones.

She yanked his sword free and handed it to Lady Thea.

When she spun to see how Jack fared, she found that he had the guard on the ground, clutching at a gash on his leg that was spurting blood. Jack disarmed him and then jerked the cloth from his own head and tied it around the man's leg.

"What's going on here?" Jack demanded.

The man was sobbing in pain. "We serve Lord Fendrel. He's been trying to start a war between Duke Peyton and Baron Longmire."

"Why?"

"I wouldn't know, would I?" The man groaned. "Oh, my leg. You've crippled me."

The expanding puddle of blood on the floor told Mara the man was more than crippled. Without a surgeon, there was no way a man could survive a wound like that.

"I'm sorry," Jack said. His face paled, and his gaze met Mara's. She knew that he had never killed a man before. It was an experience no one could ever forget.

Jack turned to the Lady Thea and her maids. "We need to get you to safety," he said.

"We'll be safe here," she said. "But you need to find Lord Fendrel and stop him."

"Where are the Duke's army and his guards?" Jack said.

"Lord Fendrel came back four days ago," Lady Thea explained, "saying they had been ambushed by the Baron Longmire's men, whom they found raiding in the western foothills. They said the Baron had kidnapped my brother, so the guard rode out to protect the villages and to search for Peyton."

"Peyton's safe," Jack said. "We tracked him to Waterstone Manor. Apparently, Lady Alicia was determined to marry him."

"What?" Lady Thea said, a smile dawning on her face. "They're married?"

Jack grinned. "Five days ago," he said. "It was a rough courtship, but he didn't seem to mind."

Lady Thea beamed at him, clearly pleased.

Jack took a deep breath and glanced at the guards. "We'll take these two out of here. You ladies lock the doors and windows after we leave."

Jack and Mara dragged the guards down the hallway and into one of the ewery closets. They tied them up and left them. Mara didn't like leaving the man with the injured leg to die, but they didn't have a choice.

"We need to find the steward first," Jack said. "If Lord Fendrel is bent on starting a war, he'll want to control Lord Dain."

Lord Dain's chambers were next to the Duke's, but Jack didn't approach them from the hallway. He led Mara through the Duke's bedchamber and into his study. Raising his finger to his lips, he stepped to the door that connected the Duke's study with Lord Dain's rooms and slid a panel to the side. The sound of animated voices reached them.

Jack moved aside and let Mara peer in. Lord Fendrel and Lord Dain stood over a broad desk with a map on it.

"You've bungled this entire affair," Lord Dain said.

"How was I supposed to know that some amorous wench would send her thugs to kidnap him?" Lord Fendrel snapped. "You were the one who was supposed to manage his love affairs."

"Lord Dragos is no fool," Lord Dain said. "He'll see through this charade soon enough, and then what are you going to do? Call your

The Deadly Jest

silly Order of the Rook to come save you?"

Mara jerked her head back from the peephole to stare open-mouthed at Jack. He scowled at her. A hollow pit expanded in her stomach. Had she been sent as a diversion for a more devious plot? Were the masters simply using her like some expendable pawn?

"Don't you dare," Lord Fendrel growled.

"What?" Lord Dain yelled. "Defy your silly Order? All you do is run around and interfere in everyone else's affairs. You feed off of chaos. I gave you a chance to bring some stability to a divided kingdom, and you go and botch a simple coup."

Jack burst into the room. Mara stumbled after him, surprised by his sudden movement. The two men spun, astonishment on their faces. Lord Dain's face paled until he realized that it was only Jack. Lord Fendrel narrowed his eyes as his gaze rested on Mara.

"I knew you were no maid servant," he said.

Jack drew his sword. The muscles rippled at his jaw. "Traitors," he spat.

"Guards!" Lord Fendrel called. The door burst open, and two men entered. "Seize them," he ordered.

The guards rushed them, but Jack was already moving. He leapt up onto the table, did a spinning kick that landed solidly on Lord Fendrel's face, and then bounded toward Lord Dain.

Mara jerked her fighting sticks from their sheaths and intercepted the guards. Her sticks whirled as she ducked inside the reach of their swords and delivered a flurry of strikes to legs, arms, and chests.

The men howled in pain but kept after her as she ducked under a table. They crashed into it, knocking over the candles that burned there. The candles ignited a small fire in the papers, but she couldn't worry about that.

One of the guards came around the table and lunged for her with a dagger in his hand. Mara cracked a stick on his wrist, his throat, his collarbone, and then ducked to attack his knees.

By then, the other guard had slipped under the table, and Mara whirled to kick him in face. He grabbed her foot and jerked her off her feet. She let him drag her toward himself. Then she slipped her stick behind his neck, crossed her arms in front of his throat, and pulled with all her strength.

The man let go of her and struggled to loosen her grip on the stick. He shoved both hands into her belly and pushed down with all of his strength. The air rushed from her lungs, but she held on.

His face burned red. His lips turned purple. He pummeled her head with his fists, but his blows were feeble. Then his full weight fell on top of her.

Mara continued to squeeze for a few seconds longer to make sure he was unconscious. She shoved him aside and scrambled to her feet, struggling against the panic of her spasming lungs. She leaned on the table as her lungs sucked in the air that was now filled with smoke.

Sweat dripped from her face. Her bruises throbbed as she tried to assess the situation.

Jack had Lord Fendrel on the ground. Lord Dain cowered behind an overturned table and watched with wide eyes until his gaze shifted to the burning table.

Terror leapt into his face, and he lunged for the table, scattering documents everywhere. He snatched up a little scroll and raced for the door.

"Jack!" Mara yelled in warning.

Jack saw the fire and leapt for the pitcher of water on the table beside the basin. But that wasn't what Mara meant.

Lord Dain was escaping with the letter.

Mara tore after him, trying to ignore the burning in her lungs and the painful cut on her ribs. Warm blood soaked her tunic. She had to get that letter.

People had come out into the hallways, and Lord Dain shoved them aside. Someone tried to grab Mara, but she whacked him with the fighting sticks and sped on. Lord Dain leapt down the stairs two at a time before he jerked open one of the hidden doors into the servants' hallway and raced toward the kitchen. Mara sprang after him.

He had longer legs, and he was outdistancing her. She would never catch him. In desperation, Mara drew back one of her fighting sticks and threw it with all the strength she could muster.

The stick cracked against his legs. He tripped and sprawled.

Mara leapt onto his back, slipped the other stick around his throat and pulled him into a choke hold. He struggled and bucked, trying to dislodge her, but she rammed her knee into his back and strained as hard as she could.

The Deadly Jest

When he fell limp, she let his head drop. She jerked a chord from her pockets and tied his hands and feet. Then she snatched up the scroll and unrolled it.

It was the letter signed by the Duke.

Mara considered running back to tell Jack that she found it, but she was afraid something else might happen and she would lose the document. Instead, she raced to her room under the stairs where she had stashed a quill and ink and sheets of paper for just such an emergency. She copied down the words as quickly as she could. Her eyes widened as she wrote. The Hallstat of Morcia had negotiated an alliance with the Dunkeldi for an all-out assault on the Kingdom of Coll. Raiding and piracy were fairly common, but full-scale invasions of neighboring kingdoms seldom happened. No wonder the Order was anxious to get its hands on this document.

Mara dusted the copy, rolled it up, and stuffed it into a pocket on her cloak. Then she dashed off in search of Jack.

Mara found Jack hunched over a basin in the great hall washing the blood and grime from his face. Lord Fendrel was hogtied in a corner, as were two dozen men wearing the Baron of Longmire's colors. Soldiers wearing the Duke's green colors, swarmed the place, searching for any more conspirators. Mara hadn't heard them arrive.

Lady Thea and her ladies tended to the wounded, while Lady Erica sprawled in a cushioned chair, carrying on in a fit of hysteria. Mara considered the contrast between the two women. Lady Thea sought to ease other people's suffering, while Lady Erica spread the suffering around so liberally that everyone within earshot couldn't help but be pained.

Jack grinned up at Mara, squeezing water from the rag over the cut on his head. Bloody water slipped down his neck to soak his shirt.

"You look satisfied," Jack said.

Mara smiled and held out the scroll.

"You'll find the steward hogtied in the hallway by the kitchen," Mara said. "He's alive."

Jack reached to take the scroll when his gaze fell on her blood-soaked tunic.

"You're injured," he said, lunging to his feet.

"It's a scratch," Mara said. Though the cut still burned, it was shallow and nothing to worry about yet.

Jack frowned as if he didn't believe her. He took the scroll and sat back down. "I never thought Lord Dain would betray the Duke."

"I still don't understand what they were after," Mara said. "They didn't really think they could just kill the Duke, did they?"

Jack shook his head. "I don't know."

He jerked a thumb toward Lord Fendrel. "He won't say anything other than that the Order of the Rook will not take kindly to the way he has been treated."

Jack studied Mara for a moment. "Do you know him?"

Mara shook her head. The Order was vast and secretive, and it disturbed her that someone from the Order had been sent to interfere in her operation. What could it mean?

Mara strode over to where Fendrel sulked with his hands tied behind his back. He gazed up at her with a smirk that made her want to slap it off his face.

"What do you think you're doing?" she demanded. "You interfered with an Order operation."

"You aren't the only one who received orders, sweetheart," Fendrel spat. "And whether you know it or not, the Order doesn't revolve around you."

Mara balled her fists. "Nor does it revolve around you. I will be reporting you to the Grand Master."

Fendrel grimaced. "Please do, my dear," he said. "I don't want to spend any more time in the Duke's dungeons than is necessary."

Mara considered demanding that he tell her who ordered him to interfere, but she knew he would never divulge the secret and certainly not in front of all these people.

She whirled away to find Jack standing behind her. She grabbed his hand and pulled him away. Jack returned to his seat and picked up the rag.

"He's a snake in the grass," Mara said.

"That's what people say about all the members of the Order," Jack said.

Mara sighed. "Just tell me what else is going on."

"Well, we just received word from a messenger from Waterstone that Duke Peyton and Lady Alicia will arrive tomorrow," Jack said.

The Deadly Jest

"And the Duke's captain figured out the whole Longmire thing was all a ruse and came back—just in time." He gestured to all the men wearing the Duke's green surcoat with the white tree on it.

"Did you tell them about the two men in the ewery closet?"

"Yeah, and I just sent someone to collect the steward. I wouldn't want anyone to think he was one of Lord Fendrel's victims and let him loose."

Mara nodded and shifted her feet. "I have to go," she said.

Jack dropped the rag and came to his feet. All the boyish silliness left his face.

"When will I see you again?" he asked.

Mara pinched her lips tight and shook her head. "I don't know," she said. "I have to get the letter back to the Order and find out what's going on. Something's wrong."

Jack shifted his feet and then stepped up to her. "You will come back. Won't you?" he asked.

Mara blinked rapidly and resisted the urge to step away. Jack's honey-colored eyes were so inviting. She had never had anyone look at her that way before. He cared about her. He wanted her to stay with him.

"I…" she tried, but could say no more. Jack pulled her into a quick kiss and then released her as if he were afraid she might punch him again. When he pulled away, a crooked smile twitched at the side of his mouth.

"We're still betrothed," he said.

Mara rolled her eyes, took one last look at him, and turned away.

Jack grabbed her arm. "I meant what I said," he whispered. "I'll miss you. Please come back."

"I will," Mara said and left.

An unfamiliar warmth filled her chest. Is this what it felt like to love?

Mara stood on the pier at Royan, waiting for the call to board the ship that would carry her back to the isle of Nairn. The clamber and chaos of the wharf crashed in her ears. The smell of fish and tar filled her nostrils. Her mind wandered to Muckle Jack and his antics. She had never met anyone like him, so full of life and mischief, and yet so loyal and brave. What she wouldn't give for a mother who could tell her what these feelings meant—and explain what she was supposed to do with them.

Someone stepped up beside her, and she instinctively pulled away, while slipping her hand to the hilt of a knife. Arno smiled down at her.

"What are you doing here?" she asked.

"You've been brooding," he said. Then he pulled her into a warm embrace. "I'm glad you're safe," he whispered into her ear. He released her and held her at arm's length. "I'm sorry I sent you into that."

Mara swallowed the knot in her throat. Arno wasn't normally this affectionate.

"I'm all right," she said.

"Did you get it?" Arno asked.

Mara patted the pocket of her cloak. "Of course." Then she frowned. "Did you know another member of the Order was sent to destabilize Morcia and take the letter before I could get there?"

A shadow passed across Arno's face, and he frowned. "No," he said.

The call to board the ship came. He grasped her elbow and steered her toward the ship.

"I followed you and waited in Royan," he said with a mischievous grin.

"You didn't trust me?" Mara asked. In her relief at seeing Arno, she hadn't thought to ask why he was there.

"Oh, I never doubted you," Arno said. "I thought I would surprise you when you came to catch a boat to Nairn. But when it took you longer than I thought it would, I did some checking. Apparently, Lord Fendrel is a member of the Order, not just an informant. One of the masters sent him a secret order to get the papers before you could and to start a war between Duke Peyton and the Baron of Longmire. Someone wants Morcia so divided that it will not be able to invade Coll or so that it can be easily split apart. I don't know which."

"But why?" Mara said. "How does the Order benefit from that?"

Arno shook his head. "I don't know. And that's what has me worried."

The Deadly Jest

They climbed up the plank and seated themselves on a stack of wooden crates, while the sailors prepared to weigh anchor.

"Did you know that ladies in Morcia can kidnap a man and compel him to marry her?" she asked.

Arno gave a gruff laugh. "It's an old practice that isn't used much anymore," he said. "On Frei-Ock Isle, it's the other way around."

"It's just sick," Mara said.

"Perhaps," Arno said. "But it does get results. You don't think the Duke was very upset by his kidnapping, do you?"

"No," Mara said. "I think he helped plan it. He used it to avoid a marriage he didn't want."

She fell silent for a moment. "Would I be able to marry—if I chose?"

Arno leaned away from her so he could see her more clearly. Her face warmed.

"Do you have someone in mind?" he asked.

"No," she said, hoping he wouldn't see her blush. "But someday I might want a family." She didn't want to tell him that her last meeting with Jack had stirred something inside her. Something she hadn't known was there.

Arno draped an arm around her shoulder. "We're your family," he said.

"You know what I mean," she said. But she wasn't sure he did. Maybe the Order had been all that Arno had ever needed.

The ship edged away from the dock as the men in the rowboat out in front heaved on the oars, and men with long poles pushed off from the dock.

Arno stared at the coastline of Morcia. "I have a feeling we're both going to be back here soon," he said. "Something is afoot."

Mara followed his gaze to the red-tiled roofs and stone towers of the city. Would she come back? Her whole life she had dreamed of becoming a full member of the Order of the Rook. Now she had done it, she didn't know what else to strive for.

Maybe she would come back to visit Muckle Jack and his dog. Perhaps she would go in search of information about her parents. Find out who she was. Maybe she wouldn't be given the choice.

War would soon sweep over Frei-Ock Mor. Morcia was unstable. Conflict stirred in the bowels of the Order. The world seemed poised to shift under her feet. All she could do was wait.

AUTHOR'S NOTE

J wrote *The Deadly Jest* because I needed to know more about Mara, who appears in Book V and will play a role in the other books of the series. I also needed to understand the Order of the Rook, which appeared officially in Book III for the first time.

Most readers will have missed its appearance in Book I. Airic, the trader that Brion, Neahl, and Redmond rescued from the bear, also belonged to the Order. He had been carrying a copy of the letter Mara secured to warn King Geric of the invasion by the combined forces of the Hallstat and the Dunkeldi. He never delivered the message because he was killed by a Taurini ambush. Neahl recovered the letter, together with the full plans for the invasion, and carried it to King Geric.

To explore Mara's character, I sent her on a mission that forced her out of her comfort zone and challenged her skills and ingenuity. Though Mara's character is complete fiction, Muckle Jack and the kidnapping and marriage of Duke Peyton both have authentic historical roots.

Jesters, also called "fools," were a common feature of medieval courts. They evolved out of the traveling minstrels and performers who were skilled in storytelling, juggling, tumbling, and telling jokes. Some were itinerant, meaning they traveled from place to place. Others were permanent employees of noble families. Their job was to entertain the court while at meals or at celebrations. They often served as social critics who made fun of the political hierarchies and personal foibles of their societies, much like our modern comedians. Jesters came from a variety of backgrounds, but some of the most

The Deadly Jest

famous had the condition known as dwarfism.

Muckle Jack in this story does not technically have dwarfism, but he is small in stature and is modeled loosely on Jeffrey Hudson (1619- c.1682), who was presented to Queen Henrietta Maria, wife of Charles I of England, in 1626, by bursting out a large pie. He became a jester for her household until the English Civil War, in which he was named Captain of Horse, and he may have seen combat.

After the war, Hudson refused to play the role of jester any longer. When a man made a joke about his height, Hudson challenged him to a duel and shot him in the forehead. Hudson was exiled for this act because dueling was illegal in France at the time, and he spent twenty-five years as a captive of Barbary pirates before he returned home to England, where he died around 1682. Charles I also employed a jester named Muckle John, about whom little is known.

Bridenapping, or marriage by abduction, has been a common practice in patriarchal societies with strong taboos against sex and pregnancy outside of marriage. Lower class men who could not afford to pay the bride price to the woman's family often engaged in the practice. Sometimes the abduction was consensual. Often it was not. As usual, women and children have suffered—and continue to suffer—most from these practices.

In *The Deadly Jest*, I turned this practice on its head to complicate Mara's efforts to complete her mission. However, it should be remembered that bridenapping still occurs in many parts of the world in which women and girls are abducted and raped, so they can be forced into marriages they do not want.

ABOUT J.W. ELLIOT

J.W. Elliot is a professional historian, martial artist, canoer, bow builder, knife maker, woodturner, and rock climber. He has a Ph.D. in Latin American and World History. He has lived in Idaho, Oklahoma, Brazil, Arizona, Portugal, and Massachusetts. He writes non-fiction works of history about the Inquisition, Columbus, and pirates. J.W. Elliot loves to travel and challenge himself in the outdoors.

Connect with J.W. Elliot online at:
www.JWElliot.com/contact-us

Books by J.W. Elliot
Available on Amazon and Audible

Archer of the Heathland
Prequel: *Intrigue*
Book I: *Deliverance*
Book II: *Betrayal*
Book III: *Vengeance*
Book IV: *Chronicles*
Book V: *Windemere*
Book VI: *Renegade*
Book VII: *Rook*

Worlds of Light
Book I: *The Cleansing*
Book II: *The Rending*
Book III: *The Unmaking*

The Ark Project
Prequel: *The Harvest*
Book I: *The Clone Paradox*
Book II: *The Covenant Protocol*

Heirs of Anarwyn
Book I: *Torn*
Book II: *Undead*
Book III: *Shattered*
Book IV: *Feral*
Book V: *Dyad*

The Miserable Life of Bernie LeBaron
Somewhere in the Mist
Walls of Glass

If you have enjoyed this book, please consider leaving an honest review on Amazon and sharing on your social media sites.

Please sign up for my newsletter where you can get a free short story and more free content at: www.JWElliot.com

Thanks for your support!

J.W. Elliot

Writing Awards

Winner of the New England Book Festival for Science Fiction 2021 for *The Clone Paradox (The Ark Project,* Book I*)*.

Award Winning Finalist in the Fiction: Young Adult category of the 2021 **Best Book Awards** sponsored by American Book Fest for *Archer of the Heathland: Windemere.*

Award-Winning Finalist in the Young Adult category of the 2021 **American Fiction Awards** for *Walls of Glass.*

Award-Winning Finalist in the Science Fiction: General category of the 2021 **American Fiction Awards** for *The Clone Paradox (The Ark Project,* Book 1).

Chet Kevitt Award for contributions to Weymouth history for the publication of *The World of Credit in Colonial Massachusetts: James Richards and his Daybook, 1692-1711.* Awarded by the Weymouth Historical Commission, 2018.

Writers of the Future Contest
    Honorable Mention for *Recalibration*, 2018.
    Honorable Mention for *Ebony and Ice*, 2019.

Printed in Great Britain
by Amazon

36491708R00088